The world is full of wishes. Secret wishes, birthday wishes, wishes scribbled in diaries, wishes mumbled to no one. Most wishes are merely words. *I wish I didn't have school tomorrow. I wish I were rich. I wish I could just disappear.* But some wishes are more than that. Some wishes, with help, can come true.

Praise for The Collectors series

Schneider Family Award Honor Book

Minnesota Book Award Finalist

"Original, brave, and addictive."—Adam Gidwitz, bestselling author of the Newbery Honor Book *The Inquisitor's Tale*

"Inventive, engrossing, and wonderfully strange."
—Anne Ursu, author of *The Lost Girl*

"Everything a young reader could wish for!"
—Jonathan Auxier, *New York Times*–bestselling author of *Sweep*

"A gentle, triumphant reminder that being different doesn't correspond to weakness."—*Publishers Weekly*

"Warm and enchanting."—*Kirkus Reviews*

"Well-written characters, expanding mythology, action-packed moments, breathtaking magic, and heartwarming friendships."—*Booklist*

The Collectors

A Storm of Wishes

JACQUELINE WEST

GREENWILLOW BOOKS
An Imprint of HarperCollinsPublishers

A Storm of Wishes
Copyright © 2019 by Jacqueline West
First published in hardcover in 2019 by Greenwillow Books;
first paperback edition, 2020.

The text of this book is set in 10-point ITC Stone Serif.
Book design by Paul Zakris

Library of Congress Cataloging-in-Publication Data

Names: West, Jacqueline, author.
Title: A storm of wishes / Jacqueline West.
Description: New York, NY : Greenwillow Books, an imprint of HarperCollins Publishers, 2019. | Series: [Collectors ; 2] | Summary: "Eleven-year-old Van Markson embarks on a quest to rescue his best friend from a dangerous wish collector"— Provided by publisher.
Identifiers: LCCN 2019012390 | ISBN 9780062691736 (pbk ed.)
Subjects: | CYAC: Wishes—Fiction. | Magic—Fiction. | Collectors and collecting—Fiction. | Best friends—Fiction. | Friendship—Fiction. | Hearing impaired—Fiction. | People with disabilities—Fiction. | BISAC: JUVENILE FICTION / Fantasy & Magic. | JUVENILE FICTION / Action & Adventure / General. | JUVENILE FICTION / Social Issues / Friendship.
Classification: LCC PZ7.W51776 Stl 2019 |
DDC [Fic]—dc23 LC record available at https://lccn.loc.gov/2019012390

20 21 22 23 24 PC/BRR 10 9 8 7 6 5 4 3 2 1

Greenwillow Books

For Danielle, who is there when the woods get dark

Contents

1
The Thing at the
Bottom of the Well

The thing at the bottom of the well was asleep.

It had been asleep for quite some time. The thing itself didn't know how long, because it no longer measured time at all. Light slipped into darkness, warmth dissolved into cold, and the thing remained where it was, drowsing, occasionally staring out at the soggy shadows through the slit of one gray eye.

The well was ancient, dug and used centuries ago. The thing at its bottom was older still. Its great gray body stretched through the tunnels that branched from the well's shaft, filling the courses where deeper water used to run. Its claws sank in the black dirt.

People brought it offerings now and then, but the thing at the bottom of the well rarely took them. It was so vast and so old that it rarely felt hunger. It rarely felt anything at all.

But once in a great while, between stretches of sleep, something small and new would catch its eye.

Late one summer afternoon, a family came walking through the woods: a mother, a father, and a five-year-old boy. They'd had a picnic in a clearing, and now they were rambling along the overgrown paths. It was the little boy who spotted the well—the crumbling and mossy wooden roof, the circle of stacked gray stones. His mother gave him a coin. The boy tossed it into the well. In half a heartbeat, it had slipped out of reach of daylight and vanished into the deep, deep dark.

The woods rustled. The little boy's parents steered him away.

Far below, at the bottom of the well, the coin landed with a delicate *tink*. It struck a mound of other coins that had piled up above the shallow water, most of them eaten away by rust and mud and time. It lay there, glimmering against the darkness.

The world is full of wishes like this one.

Secret wishes, birthday wishes, wishes scribbled in diaries, wishes mumbled to no one. Most wishes are merely words. *I wish I didn't have school tomorrow. I wish*

I was rich. I wish I could just disappear. But some wishes—the ones made on birthday candles and broken wishbones, the ones hung on falling stars or thrown down certain deep, dark wells—are more than that.

Some wishes, with help, can come true.

The thing at the bottom of the well opened its eyes. With one huge, clawed hand, it reached for the wish glinting on the pile of coins. It scooped the wish into its toothy mouth . . . and swallowed.

Mist, thick and silvery, filled the air, rising up through the well like smoke from a chimney.

And in the forest above, a unicorn leaped from the underbrush.

It galloped past the path where the family was walking, its silver mane and tail gleaming, its hooves so swift and soft that the little boy was the only one to notice it at all.

He raced off the path after it.

His parents turned a moment too late. They shouted for the little boy. They chased after him, screaming now, trampling through the bracken. Before long there were other sounds: motors and sirens, dogs snuffling through the brush, booted feet moving in lines. By the time the little boy was found, cold and scared but safe at the bottom of a ravine, nearly two days had passed. He kept insisting, while his crying parents hugged him and the EMTs checked him over, that he had wished for a unicorn, and his wish had come true.

The thing at the bottom of the well heard all of this.

It listened distantly, indifferently, the way it watched the weak shafts of sunlight that ventured down to its tunnel before being consumed by darkness.

The thing had caused far worse trouble than this.

Digging its claws deeper into the earth, it settled back to sleep.

2
Watch Out

Far away from that deep, misty forest, on one shady street in a big, bustling city, there sat a very small boy named Van.

The boy's full name was Giovanni Carlos Gaugez-Garcia Markson, but nobody called him that. His mother, the famous opera singer Ingrid Markson, called him Giovanni. Nearly everyone else called him Van, if they spoke to him at all.

At that moment, Van was seated on the broad stoop of a grand, gray stone house. Van lived there for now. But the house was not his house. Van was much more comfortable outside it, even though he could still feel the house looming behind him, its four stories of windows staring down at him disapprovingly. Inside the house, his mother was practicing a new song cycle, her powerful voice ringing through the walls. Van couldn't hear this. He'd taken out his hearing aids and left them in his bedroom when the practicing started. This was the best thing about being hard of hearing, as far as Van was concerned: it was like being able to plug your ears with your fingers but still have both hands free. Plus, without your hearing aids, you had a good excuse for not talking to anyone, which was very handy when you had no one to talk to anyway.

It was Van's own fault that they had to live in this snooty house. The house belonged to Charles Grey, director of the largest opera company in the city and Ingrid Markson's sort-of boss, as well as her sort-of maybe-almost boyfriend. Mr. Grey was wealthy and arrogant and important—or at least he was important to people who liked opera, who were the only people Mr. Grey cared about.

Several weeks before, when Ingrid was hit by a car and broke her leg while chasing Van through the city, Mr. Grey had offered them a place to stay while she recovered. Van knew he should feel grateful for this. But all he felt was a shaky wariness—the sense that as long as Mr. Grey was close, he should be on his guard.

He guessed this was what trout felt when they spotted a juicy worm dangling into their stream, its wormy body curved into the shape of a hook.

Mr. Grey had a twelve-year-old son named Peter, who was just a year older than Van. Peter and Van had one thing in common: they both wanted to keep their parents apart. Even though they agreed on this important thing, and even though they could sit at the same dinner table and say "Pass the bread" without glaring, Peter was definitely *not* Van's friend.

Van had had friends once.

They had crammed his life with excitement and danger. They had revealed the twinkling stashes of magic hidden in the world all around him. And then they had gone, leaving him behind, taking most of their magic with them.

Van slipped one hand into his pocket and grasped the swirling glass marble inside. The marble was proof that it had all really happened. That he'd been part of something big and strange and wondrous, at least for a little while. Van squeezed the marble tight. Then, letting go, he dragged his attention back to the Greys' front stoop.

Several acorns from the street's towering oaks lay

on the step beside him. All but one of them still had their bumpy little caps. Van nudged the acorns with caps into a group. The lone capless one was left by itself.

"Hey, Baldy," Van imagined the largest acorn snarling. "There's a dress code here. Acorns without caps aren't welcome."

The capless acorn sighed and inched quietly away.

Van scanned the grass around the stoop. A few tiny stones. More acorns. But past the base of the steps, just beyond the hedge that divided the Greys' property from the sidewalk, something glittered. Van scooted down the steps.

Half hidden by the hedge, partially buried in the shady dirt, was a bottle cap. Van tugged it free. Its edges were bent inward so that it formed a perfect bowl. When he brushed the dirt away, the bottle cap glinted like gold in the sunlight.

He set the bottle cap on the bare acorn.

The other acorns let out loud gasps.

"Can it be?" one of them whispered. "Is that the lost crown of Acornucopia?"

Van shoved the capped acorns closer.

"It is!" they exclaimed. "It's the ancient crown!"

All of them—except for the biggest one—bowed their capped heads. "Hail to the king!"

The crowned acorn looked around at the others, dazed and shy. "But . . . but I'm not a king. I'm just an ordinary acorn."

"The lost crown will only fit the rightful king of the Acornish," said one of the gathered acorns. "Hail, King!"

"Hail, King!" the other acorns echoed. And this time, even the biggest acorn bowed its cap.

Van checked the ground around the stoop for other lost treasures. Being hard of hearing meant that Van didn't hear the way most people heard. But it also meant that he noticed things other people didn't notice. He saw things that most people didn't see. A lifetime of traveling with his mother to one new place after another, and of being alone in those new places, had honed Van's imagination as well as his treasure-hunting skills. These things kept him busy. They kept him company. Sometimes they kept him safe.

And sometimes they did the opposite.

Van focused his eyes. A plastic pen cap was wedged against the edge of the sidewalk. A twist tie, a blue button, and a frayed strip of ribbon lay near the curb. And glinting in the dirt beneath the hedge was a long, narrow, silver bolt. Van knelt, thrusting his head and shoulders into the scratching branches. Behind him, unseen and unheard, a garbage truck rumbled onto the street.

Van pried the bolt out of the dirt. A perfect scepter for the Acornish King! He was scraping the grit from its silver whorls when he thought he heard a soft voice say, "Van. Hey. *Van.*"

Van halted.

He hadn't heard the voice at all. He had *felt* it, inside his head.

Which meant he must be imagining things.

His friends were gone. He was alone inside the hedge. No one was calling his name, no matter how much he wished otherwise.

Van crawled deeper into the hedge. The garbage truck rolled closer.

The voice spoke again. "Van. Van. *VanVanVan!*"

Now Van froze. Maybe he hadn't imagined the voice, after all. Because he certainly wasn't imagining the squirrel who had leaped into the twigs just above his face. The silvery, busy-tailed, anxious-eyed squirrel. The extremely *familiar* squirrel.

"Van!" squeaked the squirrel. "Sheesh! I've been

calling your name *forever*. Or for a few seconds. Probably seconds."

Joy filled Van's chest.

"Barnavelt!" He lunged toward the squirrel, twigs and leaves snapping around him. "I've missed you so much! Have you heard from Pebble? Where is she? Is she all right?"

The squirrel's round black eyes grew even wider. "Pebble?" he echoed, in a small voice. Then he shook himself, like an Etch A Sketch erasing its own drawing. "No. She hasn't—it's not that."

Disappointment dimmed Van's joy. "Then what?"

The squirrel blinked. "*What* what?"

"Why did you finally come back?"

"Oh!" The squirrel shook himself again. "To tell you to watch out."

"Watch out?" Van repeated. "Watch out for what?"

"No," squeaked the squirrel. "Just *WATCH OUT*!"

Barnavelt leaped out of sight.

Van sat back on his heels, perplexed. *Just watch out?* Had Barnavelt shown up after several empty weeks only to shout a few confusing words and disappear again?

And then, through the twigs of the hedge, Van saw the flash of sunlight on a windshield.

The truck was close enough that at last he could hear it too. The roar of the engine. The shriek of tires as it swerved up over the curb, coming straight at him.

Van dove backward through the hedge. He landed on his back, on the little paved patio surrounding the Greys' stoop, with one foot snagged on an ornamental yew and the other in a giant stone tub of geraniums. Leaves and twigs rained down around him. A piece of trash—one small square of paper—fluttered free of the swaying bushes and settled directly on his chest.

The truck crunched through the hedge's other end. It veered over the spot where Van had knelt a second ago, then swerved sharply, tires screeching, and disappeared from Van's view.

There was an air-bending, world-rattling *BOOM*.

A jumble of other noises followed: glassy clinking noises, rocky crumbling noises, the sharp note of a scream.

Cautiously, Van sat up. He grabbed the piece of paper that had landed on his chest and peered around the edge of the still-shaking bushes.

A garbage truck appeared to be visiting the house next door.

It had flattened several bushes before barreling straight into the neighbors' front window. The truck's cab thrust through the frame where glass should have been. Its body stuck out awkwardly into the front yard, like an elephant halfway through a too-small door. Black tire tracks streaked the pavement just in front of Van's toes.

It had all happened too fast for Van to be truly scared. What he felt was closer to disbelief, like he'd just watched the world perform an extremely messy magic trick. He swayed on the sidewalk, taking quick, hard breaths. Without really seeing it, Van glanced down at the paper in his hand. It was a tattered old postcard. The only words written on the back were WISH YOU WERE HERE.

Wish . . ., Van thought.

And then, before any passing cars could stop, before any neighbors could rush out of their houses to find out what on earth had happened, Van noticed something else.

A shimmer hung in the air. It was silvery and shifting, like dew that evaporated before it could quite touch the ground. It brushed the tips of Van's hair. By the time he blinked, it was gone.

Only Van saw that shimmer. And only Van knew what it was.

It was a granted wish.

Someone had wished to hurt him. Or worse. And the wish had been just a few inches—and one squirrel—away from coming true.

3
Curses

"We must be *cursed*!" Ingrid Markson's voice made the crystal chandelier tremble. "Someone tell me what I've done to bring these *disasters* upon us!"

Van's mother was perched on the edge of the Greys' striped silk couch, clutching Van tightly to her side. Even if he hadn't been close enough to hear every ringing word, Van could have felt them in the reverberations of her rib cage. He guessed that being hugged by Big Ben would have felt a lot like this.

"Oh, *caro mio*! *Why* is this happening to us?" His mother squeezed Van even tighter, her voice cresting with emotion. Ingrid Markson could make a grand operatic scene out of anything. Van had seen her do it in hospitals, in hotels, in busy restaurants. It may not have made a situation better, but it certainly made it splashier. "First I'm run down by a speeding car, and weeks later, my only child is nearly struck by a *sanitation vehicle!*" She stared down at Van, her eyes shimmering with dramatic, but genuine, tears. "What have I done to deserve this?"

One of the two police officers in the Greys' living room said something—something that sounded to Van like *Monsters have armed the trap.* No, he told himself, shoving back a jolt of fear. She'd probably said . . . *Must not have heard the truck.* That was all. Nothing worse.

"Yes. Giovanni is hard of hearing," said his mother weepily. She looked down at Van's ears. "And you weren't even wearing your hearing aids? Outside, in the middle of the day? Oh, Giovanni, *why*?"

Van took a breath. It was hard to explain how taking out the hearing aids could feel—the way it let him turn off his blurry hearing and focus his vision on a quiet, clearer world. But before he could even try, Mr. Grey strode in with a cup of hot tea on a saucer.

"Don't worry, Ingrid." Mr. Grey reached down to grasp her non-Van-bearing shoulder. ". . . Get to the bottom of this."

". . . May already have," said the police officer. Van

caught some of her words through his mother's sobs. ". . . Swarm of wasps . . . side the truck. The driver . . . badly stung . . . he lost control of the vehicle."

"Is he all right?" Van asked.

"Looks like he will be," said the officer. "Eventually."

". . . Lucky no one else was hurt." The second officer looked straight at Van. "And you brought the danger on yourself."

Van's heart stumbled.

No. *Angry wasps are dangerous stuff.* That was what he'd said. Everyone else was nodding, talking about how the smell of garbage had drawn the swarm. None of them suspected what Van already knew.

That those wasps had been *wished* there.

"You're safe, thank goodness," wailed his mother, pulling Van so close that his cheek smooshed upward and squeezed his right eye shut. "But how many disasters can two people endure?"

With his open eye, Van peered out the front windows. The street was in chaos, crowded with flashing police cars and tow trucks, gawking people and cordoned traffic. Nowhere in the mess did he spot a silvery squirrel.

But Barnavelt *had* been there. Hadn't he?

"Ingrid." Mr. Grey's voice pulled Van's attention away from the window. The director clasped his mother's hand, murmuring something Van couldn't catch, before turning toward Van. "And poor Giovanni." His voice was so pitying it made Van's teeth hurt. "Thank goodness you're all right."

The front door opened, letting in a burst of noise. Peter Grey and the nanny, Emma, stepped across the foyer to the doorway of the front room.

The nanny gazed around, wide-eyed. "My gosh— what happened? Is everyone okay?"

While Mr. Grey explained, and Emma rushed to give Van a hug, Peter stood with his tennis racket in the doorway, staring in at the rest of them with his chilly blue eyes.

Finally Mr. Grey said, with a sharpness that even Van could catch, *"Peter."*

"Got your way," mumbled Peter.

Glad you're okay, Van translated in his mind. That was probably what Peter had said. But Peter still didn't move any closer.

After the police officers had left, and after the delivery pizza had arrived, because no one could concentrate on cooking, they all gathered around the dining table. Peter was quieter than usual. Mr. Grey talked even more than usual. Van's mother laughed a lot less than usual. But Van only half noticed these things. His attention was fixed on the windows that gazed out over the walled backyard.

The summer evening had grown red and dim. Thickening shadows pooled behind every tree. Van was sure that if he just watched patiently enough, somewhere in those shadows, he would spot the flash of a tufty silver tail.

But there was no flash.

Peter finished eating quickly and stalked away.

After another bite, Van asked to be excused too.

His mother held out her arms. "Come here, *caro mio.*" Van let her wrap him up in a lily-scented hug. "*Nothing* matters more to me than you do. You know that," she said, her face close to his. "I will find a way to keep you safe. I promise."

Van nodded, aiming his eyes at the floor.

His mother hadn't brought the disasters upon them. *He* had. It was his fault that they weren't safe right now. It was his fault that his mother was still walking with a crutch. It was his fault that they were stuck in this stuffy house. It was even his fault, in a way, that a garbage truck had barreled through the neighbor's front windows.

Van let his mother give him one more squeeze. Then he trailed up the winding stairs and along the hall to his borrowed bedroom. After closing the door and changing into his pajamas, Van pulled a large, sturdy box out from under the bed.

Van had been building his collection for years. Everywhere his mother's singing took them, he found treasures to add to it: foreign coins and skeleton keys, model cars and dinosaurs, broken jewelry, interesting buttons, the tiny toys that tumbled out of vending machines. All the things that other people lost or dropped or didn't notice in the first place.

But Van noticed.

He dragged the collection box close to his model stage. Van's father, a set designer who now lived somewhere in Europe, had built the stage years and years ago. It was a perfect replica of a real stage, complete with working velvet curtains and a proscenium arch. Van couldn't quite remember his father, and you can't really miss something that you don't remember. But the model stage had been a part of his life for as long as he could remember anything at all.

With careful hands, Van dug through his collection. He pulled out a small china squirrel—a squirrel that he had stolen from Peter's bedroom months ago—and set it in the center of the stage. Van wasn't in the habit of stealing his treasures. The stolen squirrel still gave him a twinge of guilt, but it was so faint that he could barely feel it at all, like the yellowish splotch a bruise leaves just before it disappears for good. Next to the squirrel, he placed an action figure with a long black cape.

SuperVan.

"Barnavelt!" Van imagined SuperVan saying, in his booming voice. "It's good to see you again!"

"SuperVan! We've all missed you so much!" squeaked the squirrel. "I have an important message for you. It's about Pebble. Of *course* she hasn't forgotten about you. She *needs* you. She—*EEEEEEEEE!*" The squirrel's squeak turned to a scream.

Stomping onto the stage was the one-armed model robot Van had found in an Austrian airport bathroom.

Barnavelt let out a last squeak. "Look out, SuperVan!" The squirrel dove to safety behind the rear curtains.

SuperVan whirled to face the newcomer.

"MESSAGE REJECTED," announced the robot. "SUPERVAN: PREPARE TO FACE MY BEE-BEE GUN."

It aimed its metal hand. Before it could fire a swarm of robot bees, SuperVan launched into the air. The figurine dove close to the collection box, cape billowing heroically. It hooked its plastic arm through the coils of a miniature Slinky. Then SuperVan soared back over the stage, aimed carefully, and dropped the Slinky. Its coils fell neatly around the robot, holding it like a caterpillar in a cocoon.

"MISSION FAILED," announced the robot. "BUT SUPERVAN WILL NOT WIN AGAIN."

"We'll see about that," said SuperVan. With a quick kick, the figurine sent the robot and its metal cocoon rolling over the lip of the stage.

"AAAAAAHHH," screamed the robot.

"Hooray!" cheered the squirrel, hopping out of its hiding place. "You did it, SuperVan! You survived the robot bee attack!" It scampered adoringly around SuperVan's black plastic boots. "Now, for that message from Pebble . . ."

Van trailed off.

He set the squirrel down on the stage's black boards.

He couldn't imagine a message from Pebble. He couldn't imagine where she had gone. And he couldn't imagine what she hoped Van would do—if she still had any hope in him at all.

Van shoved his collection back into its place. Then he switched off the light, pulled back the covers, and climbed up onto the big guest room bed.

But he wasn't going to stay there.

4

Voices in the Dark

Van lay on his side, watching the gap below his bedroom door.

His mother and Mr. Grey often stayed up late together, an occasional note of his mother's laughter floating up from the living room below. But tonight, much earlier than usual, a shadow flickered past his doorway—the shadow of Mr. Grey heading along the hall and up to his own bedroom on the third floor. Apparently they hadn't found much to laugh about tonight.

The hallway light winked out. Everything went still.

Van waited for as long as he could stand it, watching the digits on the bedside clock tick upward. Five minutes. Ten. Twelve. Finally, when he couldn't keep still for another second, he swung his legs out from under the blankets.

He couldn't keep waiting for the Collectors to come to him. Not when his life was obviously in danger. He needed to talk to Barnavelt or, better yet, to someone who could concentrate for more than five seconds. He needed to do *something*.

He needed to get to the Collection.

Van fit his hearing aids into place. He listened for a moment, holding his breath. The house was quiet. He grabbed the glass marble and his emergency house key from the bedside table and dropped them into the pocket of his pajama pants. After slipping on his shoes, he inched open the guest room door.

A night-light in the guest bathroom gave off a comforting glow. Emma, the nanny, must have left it on for him. It wasn't the kind of thing Mr. Grey would think of. Peter might think of it, and then switch it off on purpose.

Gratefully, Van ventured out into the light.

He didn't like the dark.

It wasn't darkness itself that bothered him. It was the things that darkness stole from him. The dark stripped away his sharpest sense, leaving him to tiptoe into danger like a hand groping around in a drawer full of knives.

Van padded down the hallway, past the bathroom and its rosy night-light, past Peter's closed bedroom door, to the top of the stairs.

No lights shone from below. The gap below the office door was dark. To keep Van's mother from having to limp up and down the long staircase, Mr. Grey had made her a temporary bedroom in the first-floor office. She wasn't a very sound sleeper, as Van knew from experience. He hoped that the size of the Greys' house and the exhaustion of the day would keep any stray sound from waking her.

Van tiptoed down the winding steps. Below him, the foyer's dark wooden floor gleamed like a pool of oil. Van half expected it to seep up the cuffs of his pajama pants as he skidded across it toward the heavy front door.

The knob turned easily in his hand. That was odd. Maybe Emma had forgotten to lock the door when she'd left for the night. Keeping one eye over his shoulder, Van inched the door open, slipped out onto the broad stone stoop, and pulled the door shut behind him.

Someone was sitting on the steps.

Van sucked in a gasp.

The seated figure turned. By the light of the streetlamps, Van could make out its shape, its short brownish hair, its familiar face. He saw surprise and hope flare on its features for a split second before burning out.

"Oh," said Peter. "It's *you*." In the street's nighttime hush, Van could catch each chilly word.

"Did you . . ." Van faltered. "Did you think I was somebody else?"

Peter shrugged. ". . . Didn't expect *you* to come looking for me."

"I wasn't looking for you," said Van, realizing just a second too late what a nice excuse this could have been.

Peter's face sharpened into a frown. "Then what are you doing out here?"

"I was . . ." Van sorted through a dozen possible lies. He studied Peter, slumped on the steps, and moved closer until he could look directly down at Peter's face. "What are *you* doing out here?"

Peter kicked an acorn off the stoop and didn't answer.

Van's eyes moved from Peter's face to his clothes.

Peter wore a button-up shirt and jeans, even though it was very late at night not to be wearing pajamas. And there were expensive sneakers on his feet. You didn't come outside in the middle of the night, fully clothed, with your shoes on, unless—

"Are you running away?" Van asked.

"No," said Peter. Or it might have been *I don't know.* He shrugged again. "Maybe. Kind of." He looked at Van from the corner of his eye. "Is that what *you're* doing?"

"Maybe. Kind of." Van echoed Peter's words. "But I was going to come back."

Peter muttered something that Van couldn't catch.

"What did you say?" Van asked.

Peter frowned up at him. "Can't you hear me, even when you're standing right next to me?"

"Sometimes. It helps if I can see your face."

"Oh." Peter angled his body very slightly toward Van. In the streetlights, his pale blue eyes looked even icier than usual. "I said, why would *you* run away? You're the good one. The one everybody feels sorry for. Oh, poor little Van, he *almost* got hurt." He shook his head. "They don't even notice when I leave the room. They wouldn't notice if I left the whole *house.*"

Van tugged at the cuff of his pajama sleeve. Peter's

words were angry, but his voice was weaker than usual. Too weak for any of the words to sting.

"I just wanted to get out for a while," Van answered. "It feels weird, living in somebody else's house. Especially if you know you really shouldn't be there."

Peter didn't meet Van's eyes. "Where were you going to go?"

Van knew *exactly* where he was going to go. He was going to race down to the end of this street, zigzag twice, and then run for blocks and blocks until the buildings became bigger and darker, and then . . .

Van swallowed. The Collection was his secret, and he would keep it as safe and secure as the treasures in his box. He shrugged one shoulder. "Maybe back to our old apartment. Where were *you* going to go?"

There was a long pause. Van was starting to think that Peter must have mumbled an answer and he'd missed it, but then Peter kicked another acorn and said, "I don't know."

"To your mom's?" offered Van.

"My mom's gone," said Peter.

The way he said it told Van that she wasn't gone to another house, or another city, or even another country.

"Oh," said Van. "I'm sorry." He sat down on the step next to Peter. "How about your grandparents?"

"They live in England," said Peter. "And I don't really like them."

The words were so flat and factual, Van couldn't help letting out a laugh.

Peter glanced into Van's eyes for a moment. A smile pulled at one side of his mouth.

"They eat beans for breakfast," Peter went on. "Beans and stewed tomatoes. And they always send me a jar of marmalade for Christmas. That's it. Even though they're superrich. And I've never seen either of them laugh, *ever*. Not even this one time when my grandfather let out a huge fart right at the table. *I* laughed, and they sent me to my room."

Van giggled. "I suppose that's what happens when you eat beans for breakfast."

Now Peter laughed too. This made Van laugh harder. The two of them sat for a minute, their shoulders shaking, their hands clamped over their mouths.

"I don't think you should run away," said Van, when they had finally stopped giggling. "I mean—this is *your* house. My mom and I will be gone soon. I hope."

Peter shot him a look. "What if you're not?"

Van pictured this. He and his mother and Peter and Mr. Grey all stuck in the same house for weeks to come. His mother and Mr. Grey sharing more meals, laughing and murmuring, staying up together after Van and Peter had already slunk or stomped upstairs to bed.

"Maybe we should come up with a plan." Van locked his arms around his knees. "Something that would make our parents want to be apart. Or make them want *us* to be apart."

"Yeah," Peter said slowly. His eyebrows rose. "Maybe if we're so awful together—like, really loud and rude, or we mess up the whole house—maybe they'll think we're bad influences on each other, and they'll hurry and separate us."

"That's good," said Van. "What are some of the worst things we could do?"

"We could be really rude at the table," suggested Peter. "Eating with our fingers, grabbing stuff. Chewing with our mouths open. Or— Can you make yourself burp really loud? *Like this?*" he added, in a resonant burp.

"Wow," said Van. "No. I *wish*."

Peter gave a pleased smile.

Van thought for a second. "What's your dad's least favorite kind of music?"

"Death metal," said Peter instantly. "The kind where all the singers sound like Cookie Monster."

"That's perfect." Van sat up straighter. "We should pretend we're really into death metal. We should blast it all day long."

"Yeah." Peter sat up straighter too. "We could get metal band T-shirts with really creepy pictures on them. We could decorate our rooms with metal posters. We could dye our hair black!"

"Mine's already black," Van pointed out.

"Then we could bleach yours white," Peter hurried on. "And we could get those magnetic things that make it look like you pierced your nose!"

Van rocked forward onto his knees. "We could give each other fake *tattoos*!"

Peter was grinning so hard now that Van could see the streetlight glinting on his teeth. "This is a *great* plan."

Van grinned back. "I've never gotten to be a bad influence before."

"Really?" Peter's eyebrows went up. "I get called a bad influence all the time."

For a minute, they kept quiet, smiling out into the darkness together.

Then Peter said, "I guess we should get back inside."

Van's heart plummeted down to the bottom of his ribs.

Making plans with Peter had derailed his other plan—the one that took him straight to the Collection. And now with Peter waiting for him to step through the heavy front door, Van had no chance of getting that plan back on track.

"Yeah," he said slowly. "I guess."

Peter let Van pass through the door first. After locking it carefully behind them, he followed Van across the foyer and up the staircase.

"All right," whispered Peter as they reached his own bedroom door. "When should we put our plan into action?"

Van thought for a moment. "Let's say if my mom and I don't have plans to move out within the next week, we get our first death metal album."

"Sounds good." Peter flashed him a last quick grin. "Good night."

Then Peter's bedroom door swung shut, and Van was left alone in the empty hallway.

He wavered on the carpet.

Now what?

Maybe he should sneak back downstairs. But Peter was sharp-eared and currently awake; he might hear the creak of Van's footsteps. And there was the risk of waking his mother with another trip back across the first floor. Maybe there was another way out: a big drainpipe to climb, or a balcony. . . .

He was still standing in the glow of the bathroom night-light, trying to make up his mind, when he heard it.

"Van."

Van froze.

It was a soft voice, almost a whisper. Soft voices didn't always reach Van's ears, even with his hearing aids in place. But this one struck him like the needle of a dart.

Because this voice wasn't speaking to his ears at all. It was speaking straight to his mind. Had Barnavelt come back? *No,* he answered himself. The voice definitely wasn't the squirrel's. This voice had an odd quality, something that made it less like a voice and more like a *sound*—like a piece of rusty metal scraping against stone.

But it had said his name.

"Van," it said again.

The glow of the night-light revealed nothing but

bare carpet and gray walls. So the voice had to be coming from one of the bedrooms.

From *his* bedroom.

"*Van,*" it called. "*Van.*"

With a tremor in his stomach, Van stepped closer.

The voice intensified. By the time he opened the door, it seemed to echo inside his head, as though several voices were calling him at once.

He squinted into the dimness.

The room was empty. The miniature stage sat just as he'd left it. The spot where he'd lain still rumpled the bedspread. But the voices kept calling.

"*Van.*" More echoes joined in now, filling Van's head with layers of creaking sound. "*Van. Van. Van.*"

Across the room, the curtains covering the window gave one soft, slow ripple.

Van's heart hopped into his throat. He inched toward the window. Part of him wanted to turn and run away, preferably to a room with no windows and plenty of bright lights. But another, more stubborn part had to know what waited behind those curtains.

And the voices wrapped around him like fine black threads, tugging him closer. "*Van. Van. VAN.*"

He yanked the curtains aside.

Darkness.

That was all.

It filled the window from corner to corner, glossy and thick as ink.

At once, the voices went silent. Van leaned closer to the window, wondering when the sky had turned so black that it hid every hint of moon and clouds.

The darkness in the window seemed to ripple. Shifting air brushed his face.

That was when Van realized that the window was wide open. There wasn't even a pane of glass between him and the darkness.

The solid, *moving* darkness.

Before Van could back away, the darkness exploded.

Shreds of flying shadow swarmed around him. Small, needle-sharp claws snatched at his clothes. Beaks pinched the tufts of his hair. Black wings beat around his face, blurring his vision. The air whirled with birds, too many of them too count, far too many to swat away. The birds grabbed him, beaks and talons clutching his pajamas and lifting him straight up into the air. Van's feet left the floor. A second later, too surprised even to scream, he sailed through the open window, the flock of blackbirds swirling around him.

The birds carried him over the Greys' backyard. Through the blur of flickering wings, Van caught the flash of trees, a low brick wall, and then his own feet, dangling over an alley below.

As quickly as they'd snatched him up, the birds let go.

Now Van let out a shriek.

It was a short one.

Just a few feet below—about the distance from the top of a bed to the floor—the padded seat of a small, bicycle-drawn carriage waited to catch him. Van thudded into it. He sat there, gasping, too stunned to move.

Two bicycles were attached to the carriage. Each one was mounted by a man in a long dark coat. The man on the left bicycle turned around. His shoulders were broad. His face was hard. His sharp black eyes met Van's.

The man named Jack gave the tiniest of smiles. Aloud, he said, "It takes a few tricks to get hold of you, Van Markson."

Before Van could squeak out an answer, the carriage took off.

5
The Collection

The bicycle-drawn carriage sped through the city. Van rocked in its seat, pushed backward by surprise and velocity. Ahead of him, Jack and his fellow rider pedaled hard, their black coats billowing, the flock of birds wheeling around them. Jack's long, dark braid whipped in the wind.

In the short time they'd known each other, Jack had threatened Van, kidnapped him, and chased him off the side of a building—all to protect the Collection, of course. What was Jack going to do to him now? Without Pebble here to speak up for him, had Van become an outsider again? Had he turned from an ally to an enemy?

Van craned to look over the side of the carriage. It

was moving so fast, the pavement seemed to melt into gray liquid below its wheels. If he tried to dive out now, it would hurt.

A lot.

Van slid back in the seat, digging his fingernails into his palms.

Through alleyways and backstreets they raced, keeping to the darkest spots. The bicycles made a sharp right at the end of one alley, and the carriage tilted dangerously, one black-spoked wheel rising off the pavement before crashing back down. Van let out a squeak. The birds cawed.

One more turn, and the carriage rumbled into a familiar street. Van spotted the flash of the exotic pet shop's neon signs and caught the whiff of sweet dough wafting from the bakery, just before the carriage surged to a stop.

Jack swung down from his bicycle. He hoisted Van from his seat and set him on the empty sidewalk. The other rider took off. In seconds, the carriage had rounded a corner and disappeared. The flock of black birds scattered into the shadows—all except one: a huge, glossy raven, who fluttered down to perch on Jack's shoulder.

Van and Jack—and the raven—were left alone.

"Are you . . . are you kidnapping me?" Van managed. "Again?"

Jack's stony face was impossible to read. ". . . Simply cutting you," he answered.

"Cutting me?" Van squeaked.

"Escorting you," Jack repeated, more clearly. With a slightly sarcastic bow, he gestured to the building beside them.

Wedged between the pet shop and the bakery was a small, drab office building—the kind of place that was so uninteresting it practically becomes invisible. Worn wooden letters beside its door spelled out CITY COLLECTION AGENCY.

Jack opened its dingy front door. *"Inside!"* shrieked the raven on his shoulder.

Van stumbled through the doorway.

"But—what's going on?" he asked as Jack stepped past him in the office's empty blackness. "Why did you come for me now? Is this about Pebble? Is there news about her and Mr. Falborg? Or is this about that truck that almost hit me today? Do you know if—"

"Hold on," Jack interrupted.

"Hold on!" echoed the raven.

". . . Instructed to bring you here," said Jack, leading the way around a partition into an even more lightless corner. ". . . Have to wait to find out *why.*"

He flung open a hidden door.

Beyond it, a steep stone staircase angled downward.

A burst of familiar scents whirled up to Van's nose. Dust. Candle smoke. Old paper. From somewhere far below came a faint green-gold light, its glow tinging the edges of the darkness.

Jack waited until Van had stepped through the doorway. Then he shut the door soundly behind them both.

They started down the long, steep staircase. The glow brightened as they descended, washing from their feet to their knees and up to their chins, until at last they stepped out onto a wide stone floor and the green-gold light enfolded them.

Van caught his breath.

The Collection's entry chamber was even larger than he remembered. Its arching ceiling, made of greenish stone, seemed to narrow into the distance. Rows of dangling stained-glass lamps cast pools of light onto a floor as broad and gleaming as a lake. And across the expanse of that floor, Van could see the huge, open pit, surrounded by a winding stone staircase, that led down and down and down, into the subterranean dark.

The whirl of excitement and fear he'd felt on seeing this place for the very first time rushed through Van's chest, as strong as ever. But there was no time to feel it. Jack was prodding him across the floor, toward the top of that long, twisting staircase.

Van started downward. Jack and his raven marched behind.

They neared the first landing, where the words THE ATLAS were carved above a tall stone arch. Through the archway, Van glimpsed a cavernous room lit by hanging glass lamps, where people in dark coats gathered around long tables, murmuring together. Maps charting every location in the city, from public fountains to studio apartments, papered the walls. Bobbing pigeons and scurrying rats crisscrossed the floor.

Jack nudged him onward, down the stairs.

The air grew colder and damper. It seeped through Van's pajamas like water in an icy cave.

Two flights farther down, they passed another stone arch, this one carved with the words THE CALENDAR. Beyond the arch was another sprawling chamber, this one filled with bookshelves bearing row after row of identical black books. Van knew that each book was crammed with the names, addresses, and birth dates of every person in the city. Collectors needed to know who would be blowing out birthday candles, and where and when.

Gray-haired Grommet, the head of the Calendar, sat at his long desk, gathering information from the stream of dark-coated Collectors that hurried in and out of the room. Several of them brushed straight past Van on their way back onto the staircase. Only a few seemed to notice him at all. Those that did gave him small, startled looks. One woman with a rat peeking out of her coat pocket seemed to wink at Van as she passed, but she whisked onward so fast that he couldn't be sure.

"Keep moving." Jack put a forceful hand on Van's shoulder. ". . . Do than keep track of you."

"Of *you*!" taunted the raven.

They climbed downward.

Soon the air was as cold as snow. Darkness thickened before Van's eyes. The echoes of this cavernous space were beginning to play tricks on his ears, making every shuffling footstep sound like the beating of a huge wing, every distant voice seem to be coming from just over his shoulder. He gripped the banister tightly. His heart thudded harder.

They crossed another landing, turned down another steep stone flight, and reached an expanse of flat stone floor. Jack stopped him with a firm hand. Beyond this landing, the staircase twisted onward, reaching down through the chilly blackness until it met the depths of the Hold.

Just the name—the Hold—made Van shiver. He held his breath, straining to hear, but tonight, no sounds came from below. None that he could catch. Still, the roars and howls of the Creatures trapped there rang so clearly in his memory that they made his head ache.

Van turned his back on the plunging darkness.

Before him, in the largest arch yet, were carved two words: THE COLLECTION.

Jack shoved open the archway's massive wooden doors. A beam of silvery blue, like the light that glowed from an aquarium in a dark room, washed out onto the landing.

Van took a deep breath. He could feel the silvery blue of the air glittering down into his lungs. As Jack held the doors, Van crept forward, into the light.

He froze just beyond the threshold. Van had seen this chamber many times before. But the place was so huge, so strange, so *impossible*, that each glimpse of it felt like the very first one.

Van gazed around, barely breathing. A stone floor stretched away from his feet. Walls so tall that they seemed to lean inward stretched upward to a stained-glass ceiling. Spiraling iron staircases and walkways and ladders crisscrossed the chamber like thick spider-webs. In one distant corner, a mountain of coins glimmered softly. Another corner held a hill of tiny snapped bones. Dark-coated Collectors and Creatures hurried everywhere. Around them all, row upon row of shelves, more than Van could possibly count, rose toward the ceiling. Filling those endless shelves, their green and blue and indigo glass glimmering, were bottles.

And sealed in each of those bottles was a wish.

A wish made on a coin or a birthday candle. A wish made on a snapped wishbone or a falling star. A wish that had been gathered up by the dark-coated Collectors and their army of Creatures and sealed away before it could cause trouble in the world above.

When the Collectors had first explained the danger of wishing, Van hadn't quite believed them. What could be so bad about *wishes*? But after he'd seen for himself the volatile way that even the most harmless wishes could come true—like, for example, when your wish to stay in the city resulted in your mother being smashed by a rushing taxicab—Van had had to admit that the Collectors were right. About wishes, at least.

Wishes were powerful. Wishes were unpredictable. Wishes were like the fuse of a firework: a small, bright spark trailing up to a beautiful combustion.

Which could rain down from the sky and set your house on fire.

Van was still gazing up at the bottles, as still as ice, when something pounced onto his shoulder.

"Van. Van Van *Van*!"

Van turned his head to find himself nose to nose with a quivering gray squirrel.

"Barnavelt!" he gasped. "You're all right!"

"And *you're* all right!" the squirrel squeaked back. "*Are* you all right?"

"I'm fine," said Van. "Thanks to you. You got there just in time!"

The squirrel blinked. "Got where?"

"To the Greys' house. To warn me."

"The gray house?" The squirrel blinked again. "There are a lot of gray houses out there. Gray, and white, and brown, and . . . *Hey.*" Barnavelt sat up straighter. "I smell peanuts. Did you just eat peanuts?"

"No," said Van. "I—"

"Are you sure? What about peanut butter? Or peanut brittle? Or peanut—"

"You two will have to finish this fascinating conversation later," Jack interrupted. He shoved Van and his furry passenger forward. ". . . waiting for you."

With Jack's hand on his back, Van staggered across the massive floor. Flocks of pigeons scuttered out of his path. Long-coated Collectors rushed past him, labeling bottles, depositing wishes on the shelves, whisking quickly away again. As he moved through the room, Van spied the traces of recent damage: a bent iron staircase here, a broken railing there, the emptiness of several scorched, bare shelves.

He hadn't stepped inside this chamber since the night when his—unintentional—actions had nearly destroyed it. The night when Pebble disappeared. Anxiety writhed in his stomach.

Jack steered him toward the rear wall, where three Collectors were gathered in a tight huddle.

The woman with short, sleek hair and a pigeon on her shoulder was Sesame, head of the Atlas. The bearded, bespectacled little man beside her was Kernel, head of the Collection. And looming over both of them, his back to Van, was a tall, thin man with wiry gray hair.

The man turned at their approach.

High cheekbones. Steely gray eyes. Two black rats perched like epaulets on his shoulders.

Nail.

If the Collectors had a leader—and Van was pretty sure they did—it was Nail.

The Collectors' faces weren't angry. But they weren't friendly either. Van's heart plummeted like a sack down a garbage chute. Since early summer, Van had started to think of himself as *almost* a Collector. He could see wishes. He could hear the Creatures. He could do things ordinary people couldn't do. It had made him feel special—special in an included way instead of an excluded one. But there was nothing in the faces of these Collectors that said "welcome back."

So . . . why had they brought him here?

"Van Markson." Nail's voice snipped through the background noise like a pair of shears. The others went quiet.

Nail reached down and took Van's trembling hand. Van nearly jumped backward.

Nail's grip was warm. He bent lower, his face wearing something that wasn't quite a smile, but that wasn't anything else either. "We are glad you are well."

"I . . ." Van's tongue was dry as paper. "You too."

Sesame and Kernel shifted closer, staring down at Van with sharp eyes. Van couldn't meet their gazes. He felt like a moth on the end of a pin.

"Isn't this nice?" gushed the squirrel on Van's shoulder. "Everybody's back together again! Well, everybody except—" He halted. "Never mind. I mean, *she's* not who I meant. I just meant . . ." The squirrel's nose twitched. His gaze flashed away. "Does anybody else smell peanuts?"

"Let's not waste time." Nail straightened again, his black coat sweeping the floor around him like a pool of shadows. "Van Markson. We believe that Pebble may have tried to contact you."

Van jerked hard enough that Barnavelt almost slipped off his shoulder.

Just hearing her name aloud felt like a punch.

Pebble.

The girl with the sloppy ponytail and the too-big coat and the squirrel named Barnavelt on her shoulder. The girl he'd spotted scooping pennies out of a scummy park fountain. The girl he'd seen when no one else even bothered to look.

His friend.

His friend who was gone.

Everyone was waiting for him to speak. Van closed his fist around the marble in his pocket.

"I haven't heard from Pebble since she left with—with Mr. Falborg." He pushed out the words. "I haven't heard anything at all."

Nail's eyes narrowed. "Are you certain?"

Van swallowed. He glanced at Sesame and Kernel and Jack. Their faces were as still as glass.

A cold, hollow spot tunneled through Van's chest.

"I'm certain," he answered, his voice barely a whisper. "I've been waiting. I've been watching. Nothing."

"Peanuts," whispered Barnavelt.

No one else spoke.

Van tightened his grip on the marble. "What . . . what makes you think she tried to contact me?"

"Our members have seen wish activity near your current residence," Kernel explained, patting his hands together in a way that had always reminded Van of a penguin's flippers. "Aftereffects. Reality-altering mist."

"Oh." Van shook his head. "That wasn't because of

Pebble. I'm pretty sure Mr. Falborg made a wish to kill me with a garbage truck." A leftover shiver twitched down Van's arms. "He must still be trying to get rid of me."

Sesame folded her arms, tugging Van's attention upward. "You don't need to worry about your safety," she said. "There has been a rotating guard of Collectors and Creatures watching you ever since Falborg took flight."

"What? You . . . there has?" Van blinked up at the stern faces of the Collectors. Only Sesame's pigeon blinked back.

Van wasn't used to overlooking things. The thought that he had missed something so huge made him feel queasy—as though a floor he'd thought was solid had started to crumble under his feet. The Collectors were spying on him. That wasn't something you did to an ally. It was what you did to an enemy.

"So, you've been watching me every second . . . ," he ventured, "and you almost let me get squished by a garbage truck?"

"Well." Nail aimed a glance at Barnavelt. "*That* close call was the fault of one particular individual. Someone who was distracted by the smell of snack foods in your neighbors' garbage can."

Van turned back to Barnavelt. The squirrel was staring mistily into the distance, his little nose sniffing at the air. "Honey roasted," he whispered.

Behind Van, Jack gave a snort.

"If Pebble needs help . . ." Van pushed himself onward. "Why wouldn't she just contact *you*?"

"She may not be able to." Sesame inclined her head. "Falborg is certain to be keeping an eye on both her and us."

"Because the Collection is wish-proof, as you'll recall, her options for communication are limited," added Kernel.

"And, as unpleasant as it may be to consider," said Nail, in that low, clear voice that made everyone else fall silent, "there is the chance—however small—that she may have realigned with her uncle. She may be working with him against us."

"Pebble would never do that." The words shot out of Van's mouth before he could weigh them. "I was there when she left. She *had* to go with Mr. Falborg. He *wished* her to."

"Remember, Van Markson. A wish cannot force someone to do something they fundamentally would not do." Nail's voice stayed calm, but his dark eyes burned with something Van couldn't identify.

"Then you don't think Mr. Falborg is imprisoning her?" Van asked. "You don't think he's . . . he's hurting her?"

Nail bent down, bringing his face level with Van's. The rats on his shoulders sniffed at Van's breath. Van looked at their bright, beady eyes. Raduslav and Violetta. They'd once sat on his shoulders and talked to him in their tiny, ratty voices. Now even they were keeping their distance.

"Falborg takes good care of his possessions," said Nail. "He will keep her safe. He will be kind. He will try to convince her to see things his way. Remember, she has seen them his way before."

Van swallowed. He'd once seen things Mr. Falborg's way himself. Sometimes, in spite of everything he'd learned, he still did.

"If she *has* realigned with Falborg," Nail went on, "it's all the more likely that she will contact you and not us. She may try to persuade you to act on her behalf."

Van swallowed again. "So—what should I do?"

"Stay at the Greys'." Nail's voice was clear and hard, and Van knew this wasn't advice. It was a command. "Leave the house as little as possible. If you see evidence of wishes, let us know *immediately*." Nail's tone softened very slightly. He gave Van's shoulder a brief grasp. "Don't lose hope, Van Markson."

He let go of Van's shoulder and straightened to his full, towering height.

Before Van could back away, Nail spoke again.

"There is one other thing." His stare fell onto Van like a stone dropped from a bridge. "Have you seen any trace of your escaped Wish Eater?"

Every cell in Van's body froze.

His Wish Eater.

Early that summer, kindly Mr. Falborg had led Van through the twisty corridors of his home. The big white house was crammed with odd and wondrous collections: beetles behind glass, mechanical iron banks, theatrical masks, wreaths of knotted human hair. In one hidden room, Mr. Falborg had shown Van his most precious collection of all: the Wish Eaters.

The Wish Eaters were tiny, misty creatures, given refuge by Mr. Falborg before they could be trapped and exterminated by the Collectors. Mr. Falborg had given Van a Wish Eater of his own to care for: a big-eared, wide-eyed, lemurlike creature that Van had named Lemmy.

When the Collectors had captured Lemmy, stealing the little Eater from its shoebox beneath Van's bed, Van had rushed to the depths of the Collection to rescue it. But the Hold contained truths that Van hadn't expected—truths about the danger of the Eaters, and about the real aims of the Holders that trapped them. Just when Van had realized that he couldn't take Mr. Falborg's side anymore, Mr. Falborg had dragged him back on to it. Controlled by Mr. Falborg's wish, Van had released not just Lemmy, but a horde of tiny Eaters. Then he had watched, horrified, as those Eaters grew to monstrous size, feasting on collected wishes, injuring Collectors, and wreaking havoc on the Collection itself before scattering out into the city above.

But Lemmy hadn't scattered.

Lemmy had saved Van's life, pulling him from the path of an underground train, before flying off into the pale morning sky.

Afterward, left behind by his friends, Van wasn't sure where he belonged. Not with Mr. Falborg, who could be generous and kind, but also controlling and treacherous. Not with the Collectors, who kept the world safe by stealing its magic and driving creatures like Lemmy to extinction. After all, if Van hadn't released Lemmy, he wouldn't be standing here right now. He'd be as flat as a speeding train could make him.

Van wavered, not meeting anyone's eyes. He stared across the chamber at a mangled iron staircase instead. The Collectors stood silently around him.

"No," Van managed at last. "I haven't seen the Eater."

Sesame and her pigeon inclined their heads. Kernel's spectacles glittered. Behind Van, Jack loomed like a brick wall.

Nail kept silent. The rat on his left shoulder whispered into his ear.

"Very well," said Nail at last. "Jack, you may take him home." His gaze sliced to Van. "Keep your eyes sharp, Van Markson." Nail turned back to Kernel and Sesame so that his final word was muffled. But it sounded like "Beware."

Maybe Nail had said, "Be aware." Or even "Take care." It didn't matter. The warning had already tunneled straight down Van's spine, filling each bone with ice.

"Let's go." Jack's big hand wheeled him around.

Van staggered forward, half relieved, half wounded, not sure whether he was escaping or being thrown out.

"Where are we going?" asked the squirrel on Van's shoulder. "Can we stop for some peanuts on the way?

Or—wait. For some popcorn and peanuts? Or—wait. For some caramel corn *with* peanuts?"

"*We* are not going anywhere," said Jack. He signaled to his raven.

The bird dove at Barnavelt like a feathered warplane.

Barnavelt gave a squeak. He leaped from Van's shoulder onto the nearest staircase.

"Bye, Barnavelt!" Van managed to call.

"Bye, Van Gogh!" Barnavelt called back.

Jack's hand clamped tighter around Van's arm, pulling him toward the doors.

But before they could reach them, the doors swung open.

A Collector stepped into the chamber.

Jack yanked Van to the side. The raven on his shoulder cawed. Behind them, other Creatures and Collectors scattered like cars pulling out of the path of an ambulance, or like a flock of birds flying from a gun.

The Collector strode toward the podium at the center of the room. Van caught a flash of sleek black hair and a high-collared coat with a spider on its lapel as she passed.

"Who is that?" Van asked, staring after her.

Jack muttered an answer.

"A Debt Collector?" asked Van, who was pretty sure he'd heard that term before.

"*Death* Collector," said Jack. He shoved Van through the doors and into the darkness. "Anyone above dies, we take note. Because their preserved wishes die too. And dead wishes aren't something to mess with."

Van had learned about dead wishes weeks ago. Kernel had said that they were the most dangerous wishes of all, impossible to predict or control. He'd called them "pure chaos." Those words still lingered in Van's mind, pulsing with a fiery, bottled light.

Van and Jack started up the long staircase.

"What happens to them? The dead wishes?" Van couldn't help asking.

"We keep them," said Jack shortly.

"Where?"

"Somewhere safe."

"Safe!" shrieked the raven.

As he climbed, Van glanced over the banister. The black pit gaped below. He thought of all the things that were hidden down there, and all the things that *could* be hidden down there, the corridors he had never seen and locked rooms he had never entered. Then he climbed faster.

They passed the Calendar and the Atlas, crossed the expanse of the entry chamber, and hurried up the last narrow flight and out through the office of the City Collection Agency.

Outside, the night was damp and still. Fog had settled over the city. Mist draped the tops of streetlamps, turning them to giant glowing Q-tips. Buildings disappeared a few stories from the ground. The moon and stars were so well hidden, they might not have existed at all.

Van peered into the fog, wondering if a bicycle-drawn carriage was about to appear. But Jack had already turned to the left.

Jack murmured something over his shoulder—something that sounded like "Complications dooming it all." Van couldn't gather the energy or the courage to ask him to repeat it. He simply scurried after him.

They kept to the quiet streets, where cars were few and lights were dim. Jack strode along, his collar high. Van shivered in the damp air.

Soon they approached a tiny park, where lilac hedges and a few green benches encircled a small, sputtering fountain. Van caught the scent of leaves decaying in rusty water.

An old woman in a shabby sweater was passing the park on its opposite side. As Van watched, she pulled a coin from her handbag and tossed it toward the fountain. Van couldn't hear or see the coin land, but he saw the old woman close her eyes for a moment, almost as if she was praying. She turned and shuffled slowly into the darkness.

Jack raised a hand, signaling a stop.

"Lemuel," he commanded.

The raven dove across the park. It soared toward the fountain, wings slicing the fog like scissors, and flashed down toward the water. A second later, it glided back to Jack's shoulder, a gleaming coin in its beak.

Lemuel dropped the coin into Jack's palm.

"Any others?" Jack asked.

"Naw!" cawed the raven.

Van couldn't tell exactly what happened next, even though he'd seen it happen before.

As Jack touched the coin, a glow emerged from inside of it, like a golden card pulled out of a plain envelope. Jack slid the glowing wish into one of his coat's many pockets. He thrust the coin at Van. "Here."

Van looked down at the penny in his hand. It was dull and slightly damp, and it had the strange weight of something that had been alive, but wasn't anymore. He glanced toward the street where the woman had shuffled away. The reminder that wishes were pulled out of the world every day, the chances for magic stolen in wisps of candle smoke and wet coins, made the night seem darker than before. But Jack was striding onward. With heavy feet, Van followed.

He waited until Jack was passing through the beam of a streetlight before calling out, "Um . . . Jack?"

Jack wheeled around, frowning down at him. He scanned the deserted street before answering. "Yes?"

Van watched Jack's sharp face in the streetlight. "I've been wondering, and I don't know who to ask, now that Pebble's gone . . ." He touched the wish-less penny in his pocket. "Why can I see wishes and hear Creatures and notice all of you when no one else can?"

Jack gave a little snort. ". . . Been wondering that ourselves."

"Do you think—" Van pushed himself onward "—maybe—somebody in my family was a Collector, and so—"

But Jack was already shaking his head. "It doesn't work like that. You were *born*, right? You have a mother?"

"Yes. I definitely have a mother."

Jack folded his arms. "Our best guess is—it's just *you.* You notice things other people don't bother to notice, right? You see and hear a bit differently?"

Van nodded.

"Maybe that's all it is."

"Then . . . are there other normal people who can see and hear you? Like me?"

Jack looked at Van with narrowed eyes. "At least one."

Neither of them had to say which one that was. But Van knew it was a certain crinkly-eyed old man in a spotless white suit.

Ivor Falborg.

Jack turned and walked on.

At the corner of the Greys' street, he stopped. He nodded along the foggy sidewalk toward the Greys' front stoop.

"Watch for her," he muttered.

No. *I'll watch from here.* That was what Jack had said. Still, the words Van had almost heard hung on his heart like burrs. As though he had ever stopped watching for Pebble. As though he ever would.

"Good night," he whispered, because leaving in silence seemed rude.

Then he shuffled forward down the sidewalk, still rubbing the penny with his thumb.

Van reached the Greys' stoop. He'd climbed hundreds of steps tonight, but these last few were the hardest. Van dragged himself onto the first broad stair, and then paused to glance back at the street behind him.

Fog filled the air with soft gray ghosts. He could just make out the row of houses across the street, their windows dark, their lights out. The street corner was lost in fog. If Jack and Lemuel were still there, he was sure they couldn't see him either. Still, he had the sense that he was not alone. That someone was watching.

Van shuffled over the second step. An acorn crunched under his foot. Another step. The front door loomed above him like a sneer. He was about to haul himself over those last few feet when something wedged in the steps just ahead of him fluttered in the breeze. Van reached down and grabbed it.

It was the postcard that he had picked up earlier— the one that had landed on him when he made his dive through the hedge. In all the panic and screaming and hugs from his mother, he must have dropped it and not even noticed.

Van squinted down at it. On its front was a sketch

of a rambling brick building with tall, skinny windows, pointed rooftops, and a peaked tower at one end. A shadowy forest surrounded it. It looked like a cross between a college and a castle, but it was probably just some weird old hotel, Van reasoned. He flipped the postcard over. There was no name or address, not even a stamp. Just the words WISH YOU WERE HERE.

Van ran one finger over the message. Someone, somewhere, a long time ago, had written these words to someone they missed.

Van knew how it felt to miss someone. He couldn't even send a postcard to the ones he missed most.

WISH YOU WERE HERE.

Van glanced up at the Greys' unfriendly front door. He wished he didn't have to step through it. He wished both Pebble and Lemmy were with him. He wished he knew what to believe, or where he belonged.

He wished.

But he didn't have any wishes to use. And he knew better than to rely on wishes, anyway.

Van took a deep breath. Stuffing the postcard into his pajama pocket, he unlocked the looming front door and shut it again softly behind him.

Even if he had stayed on the stoop, and even if he

had looked straight up at the sky at that very moment, the heavy fog in the air would have kept him from seeing what happened next.

He wouldn't have seen the falling star streaking over the city, its flare swallowed by layers of clouds. He wouldn't have seen the tiny firefly spark that formed over the stoop where he'd stood, hovering there for an instant before floating upward, winking softly.

He wouldn't have seen a creature with a large, hazy body and wide silvery eyes emerge from the fog. He wouldn't have seen the creature float down above the Greys' rooftop, grasp the floating spark with its fingers, and swallow it. He wouldn't have noticed the shimmer that filled the air for an instant, swirling through the mist already drifting there.

Van trudged upstairs to bed.

And behind him, the world began to change.

6
Not So *Buon Giorno*

"Buon giorno, caro mio!"

Van squinted into an unwelcome beam of sunlight. Standing over his bed, as radiant as another sunbeam, was his mother.

Van's mother spoke Italian when she was especially happy. She used French when she was feeling nostalgic, and she slipped into German when she was mad. Even if Van hadn't known all of this, the smile on her face would have told him everything.

"Mom?" Van struggled to pull himself upright. He felt as though he'd spent most of the night running up and down damp stone staircases—which, of course, he had. "You're . . . upstairs?"

"Si, mio bambino caro!" His mother threw out the

arm that wasn't holding her sleek black cane. "My leg *is* almost fully healed, and I just couldn't wait to share some good news. So I brought the good news to you!"

Even though his mother's voice filled the inside of his head like a big brass bell, Van groped for his hearing aids. He didn't want to miss a single bit of what came next. Because the look on his mother's face—and the Italian—told him it was something big.

A flash of terror seared through him. Had Mr. Grey proposed? Were they getting married?

Van glanced at his mother's hands. No diamond rings. Not yet, anyway.

"What is it?" he croaked, shoving the hearing aids into place.

His mother perched on the side of the bed. She wore black slacks and an ivory silk blouse, plus a fancy necklace she'd gotten during their last stint in Santa Fe. Her coppery hair was swept up in a twist. His mother tended to dress up even when she was lying with a broken leg on somebody else's couch, but now she looked *especially* dressed up. She looked like she was going somewhere.

"Giovanni." His mother leaned closer. "Yesterday, I was desperate, sure that the two of us were cursed. But today, I'm overjoyed." She grabbed his hand in her two soft ones. "All of our problems are solved at once! New work for me, a place to live, and best of all, getting both of us out of this dangerous city!"

The terror inside Van flared up again. "What?"

"I have been offered a special position as Distinguished Coaching Artist-in-Residence"—Van could practically hear the capital letters in his mother's voice—"at the *Fox Den Opera's fall festival season*!"

"What?" said Van again.

"Fox Den is upstate—just a train ride away, but in a completely different world!" his mother sang. "It's a marvelous old estate in the country. Acres of grounds, beautiful lodging for the entire opera company, professional chefs, a swimming pool, five rehearsal halls. It's essentially *heaven*!"

The words thunked through Van's head like marbles spilling from a jar and bouncing off in all directions. Fall season. Swimming pool. *Upstate.*

"Wait," he managed. "So—we're leaving?"

"That's right." His mother's smile dimmed slightly. "As kind as the Greys have been, and as much as I hate to leave them, it's time for us to move on. This city is so big and so loud, and for someone small and special like you, *caro mio* . . ." She squeezed Van's hand. "The country will be quieter. It will be *safer.*"

Van scrambled to gather the spilled marbles. He wanted to argue, to explain that his *special* hearing had nothing to do with the danger he was in, but he could grasp only a few problems at a time. "So . . . we're leaving the city? For the whole fall?"

"For the fall. Or for good. We'll have to see what comes next!" His mother swished one hand through the air. "The Fox Den provides a tutor for company members' children, so you won't have to start another new school. We'll live there, in our very own quarters, with no busy streets or speeding garbage trucks for miles around! It will be perfect!"

Van tried to breathe, but his lungs had forgotten how.

The Collectors had told him to stay put. What if Pebble *did* try to reach him? What if Lemmy came back, lonely, hungry, and afraid? And what if Van wasn't even there?

"Mom . . . ," he began.

But the truth was one giant, complicated knot of impossible secrets. There was nothing he could even begin to unwind.

"When would we leave?" he croaked.

His mother's eyes sparkled. "Tomorrow!"

Now Van sat bolt upright. "Tomorrow! But—"

"Don't worry." His mother coaxed him back with both hands. "This is going to be the easiest move we've ever made. We'll leave our things where they are in our old apartment, pack up the stuff that we brought here, and set off! Later we'll come back for anything we need. The city is just a train ride away. A *long* train ride. But it's nothing compared to that trip from Paris to Tokyo to Sydney! Remember that?" His mother laughed. "We were so disoriented from the time changes and the jet lag, for three days we ate pizza for breakfast and had dinner at three a.m.!"

Van remembered. But he was barely listening. His thoughts were climbing out the window, leaping into the yard, and running away through the city. He had to ask the Collectors what to do. He had to let them know that he didn't *want* to leave. He couldn't give them one more reason to think he was an enemy.

His mother climbed off the bed and headed toward the closet. A limp broke the line of her usual graceful walk. Leaning on the cane, she threw open the closet door and revealed the row of Van's carefully hung clothes.

"I have to make a quick visit to the bank," she said, turning back to him. "In the meantime, you should get up, get dressed, and start packing!" She stepped toward the door. "Quick, *caro mio*! *Velocimente!*"

She swished happily into the hallway.

A moment later, Van threw himself out of bed. He wriggled into some dark clothes and hurried out into the hall.

His mother had vanished down the staircase. He could hear her speaking loudly into her cell phone, her voice ringing up from the foyer below. Van thought he caught the words "train" and "Leola" and *"domani"*—Italian for "tomorrow"—just before the heavy front door banged shut.

Van flew down the stairs. He'd nearly reached the door when a voice from behind him called, "Van! Glad I caught you."

Van whirled around, pressing his back to the door.

Mr. Grey was sauntering down the staircase, adjusting a button on the cuff of his spotless dress shirt.

What had Mr. Grey meant by *caught*? Had Peter told on him for nearly sneaking out?

". . . Hear you're leaving us," said Mr. Grey. "I hope . . . sour guess . . . too unpleasant."

Van had always found Mr. Grey's soft, accented voice hard to understand. Maybe it was because Mr. Grey always kept his face so stiff and his chin so high in the air. It often felt like Mr. Grey was speaking to some invisible person floating a few feet above Van's head.

"Yes," said Van. "I guess."

"May I speak with you for a moment?" Mr. Grey gestured to the living room.

When people like Mr. Grey asked a question like this, it wasn't really a question at all. Heart spiraling down toward his stomach, Van followed Mr. Grey's pointing arm.

He sat down on the edge of the couch.

Mr. Grey sat in an armchair opposite.

"I'll be sorry to see you go," said Mr. Grey. "But once your mother makes up her mind, there is no changing it. As I'm sure you know."

Mr. Grey gave him something that Van guessed was supposed to be a conspiratorial smile. It looked more like he was suppressing a burp.

"To be honest, I'm concerned," Mr. Grey went on. "Your mother hasn't entirely healed and traveling long distances with a child with special needs can't be easy, even for someone in perfect health."

Van bit his lips.

He could have shot back that without his sense of direction, his mother would probably *still* be wandering around the bridges of Venice. Without Van to remember their room numbers, his mother would have sashayed into a few hundred strangers' hotel rooms instead of just a few dozen. Without Van keeping track of them, his mother would have lost more keys, more gloves, more sunglasses, more cash—more of everything that could slip out of a pocket without her noticing.

Van always noticed. He and his mother took care of each other. But those stories belonged to them, and no one else.

"She . . ." Mr. Grey was continuing more quickly, ". . . taken . . . her mind . . . this *curse* . . . there's no dissuading her. She believes she must get you out of the city." He looked at Van for a long, wordless moment.

Van started to wonder if he'd missed a question. Maybe Mr. Grey's British inflection had made it sound like a statement instead. He stared at Mr. Grey's chin and waited.

The quiet curdled around them.

Van wished there was a creature of some kind in the room to break the tension. A lazy cat to pet. An unselfconscious dog rolling around on the carpet. Maybe even a distractible squirrel. But people like Mr. Grey never had pets.

Van rubbed his palms over his own knees.

If Mr. Grey would just hurry up, he might still have time to race to the Collection and back before his mother returned.

But then Mr. Grey said something that made Van forget everything else.

"She's doing this for you, you know. *Only* for you."

Van looked straight at Mr. Grey. Mr. Grey looked back at him. "For me?"

"This is *not* a move that will advance your mother's singing career." Mr. Grey's voice was as polite and careful as always, but it seemed more direct, somehow—as though Mr. Grey was finally speaking not *at* Van, but *to* him. "For the first time, she'll spend an entire season coaching other singers, not performing herself. It may not be easy for her to make a comeback afterward. It *certainly* won't be easy for your mother to step out of the spotlight." Mr. Grey paused for a moment. "But she believes that she must get you out of this city. That you'll be safer up there in the woods. Maybe she's right; maybe not. I *do* know that she is doing this solely for you. Not for herself."

Mr. Grey's words sank straight into Van's body. He could feel them settle on his heart, weighing it down like birds on a thin branch.

His mother was doing this *for him*.

Van had lost everyone else. Lemmy. Pebble. The Collectors. Mr. Falborg. None of them needed him anymore. And the problems that tangled between them weren't something that he could fix on his own anyway.

The only person left in the entire world who actually needed him was his mother.

The one who had never left him.

"What should I do?" Van whispered. "For her?"

"Keep an eye on her, please." Now Mr. Grey's voice was gentle but clear. "I know how good at that you are. And if you need anything at all, do let me know."

Van nodded. Mr. Grey shook Van's hand with a grip that was much smoother and cooler than Nail's.

Then Van got up from the couch, turned away from the front door, and dragged himself upstairs to pack.

7
In the Fox's Den

"Isn't it *lovely*?"

Van's mother spun in a circle, taking in the rooms around them. Their suite was in a converted stable, with stone walls and polished hardwood floors and wide windows everywhere. From the front of the stables, forking paths led to the Fox Den mansion and trailed across the wooded grounds to the open-air stage. To the back of the stables, there was nothing but woods.

His mother leaned on the sill of an open rear window and took a deep, piney breath. "Oh, Giovanni, we are going to be *so happy* here!"

Van couldn't find an answer in the emptiness inside him.

Like a sleepwalker, he shuffled to his mother's side.

The woods beyond the window looked damp and dense and dark, even in the daylight.

Van and his mother had lived in dozens of cities. They moved so much, his mother liked to tell people that they owned more suitcases than dishes—which was true. But Van had never lived in a place where you could look out the window and see nothing: not a single other building, not a single other window looking back at you.

The emptiness that filled him pulled harder, as though he were being swallowed from the inside.

"Didn't I tell you?" sang his mother. "It's like heaven."

Van just nodded.

The Greys had escorted them to the train station early that morning. Van had stared out the car window on the ride there, looking for one last glimpse of a familiar dark coat, or the flash of a silvery, bushy-tailed squirrel. But he'd seen nothing.

At the station, Mr. Grey and Van's mother leaned close together, murmuring words that vanished into the din. Van and Peter stood side by side, watching them. The station was so echoingly loud, and Van's eyes were focused so tightly on his mother's lips, he didn't notice

Peter trying to get his attention until Peter shouted, *"HEY!"* and bumped his arm at the same time.

". . . Too bad din . . . put our plan into action," Peter said, once Van turned to face him. "The metal bands and the burping and everything."

"Oh. Yeah." Van tried to smile, but his face might as well have turned to cement. "That would have been great."

His mother had taken hold of his arm, and the two of them had climbed aboard the waiting train. Through the windows, Van spotted Mr. Grey and Peter, still standing on the platform. Van caught Peter's eye. He managed to lift one hand and flash the devil's horns gesture, like he'd seen metal fans do. Peter grinned. A second later, the train had lurched forward, and the Greys slipped out of sight.

Now, staring out the window into a forest that seemed to go on forever, Van almost wished he was staring out at Peter Grey instead.

"I'm meeting with the company directors for a little chat," said his mother, tugging Van's attention back to the present. "Would you like to come along?"

Being alone in this place sounded terrible. But being alone among a crowd of operatic strangers sounded worse.

"I'll stay here," he said.

His mother gave him an understanding smile. Van felt an ache within his ribs, knowing that she didn't understand at all.

"This will take a little getting used to, *caro mio*." His mother wrapped an arm around him. "Give it time. I just know we're going to love it here."

She planted a kiss on Van's forehead before picking up her cane and sashaying toward the door.

"Oh, Giovanni," she added, turning back. "Stay indoors for now, until we've had the chance to explore the grounds. I'm sure we're perfectly safe, but in the woods . . . you never know." She blew another kiss. *"À bientôt!"*

The door thumped shut behind her.

For the space of a few breaths, Van stood perfectly still. The room stood still around him. There were no rumbles vibrating through the floor, because there were no apartments or hotel rooms below it. There were no tremors of traffic buzzing through the walls, because there was no traffic. There wasn't even a street. There was only the dark mass of the woods, softly swaying beyond the windows.

Van tugged the window shut.

The room grew even stiller.

He shuffled into his new bedroom. The bare walls and empty shelves gaped at him. The cover on the bed looked stiff and crackly, and Van could already tell that it wouldn't keep him warm. Turning to his pile of luggage, he unzipped the suitcase that held his miniature stage and collection box.

The train had jostled his treasures around, but nothing seemed to be broken. Van dug past model cars and plastic trees, past the wooden pawn that he'd once used as a stand-in for Pebble, past the gray china squirrel with its curling tail.

SuperVan had sunk all the way to a bottom corner. Van pulled the figurine into the light. Somehow, SuperVan looked smaller today. His gleaming black boots were duller. His little cape hung askew.

Van set SuperVan in the center of the bare black stage.

He stared at the figurine for a long time, waiting. But he couldn't think of a single thing for SuperVan to say or do.

At last he gave the figurine a little nudge. It toppled onto the stage floor. Its blank plastic eyes stared at the ceiling.

Van left it lying there.

With a deep breath, he hauled himself to his feet. As he turned back toward his pile of luggage, something outside the window glimmered.

Van whipped around.

At the edge of the forest, among the shadows and shifting leaves, there was a brief flash of silver. Van sucked in a breath. Had Barnavelt followed him all the way here? Were the Collectors still watching him, keeping him safe? Was he still—almost—one of them?

But as Van stood there, watching, not even letting his eyes blink, the edge of the forest went still. The leaves stopped their shifting. The shadows solidified.

There were no more flashes of silver. There were no distractible squirrels or watchful dark-coated figures staring back at him. What he'd seen might have been the silvery underside of a leaf—or maybe it had been nothing at all.

He waited for another minute, just in case.

Nothing.

When Van finally turned away from the window for good, he could still feel the feathery touch of eyes following him. But he knew this was only wishful thinking.

* * *

The next morning, after a night of not-quite-warm-enough sleep, Van accompanied his mother to the dining hall for breakfast.

The Fox Den mansion was a long, stately building made of gray stone, huge enough to hold one full-sized theater, two rehearsal halls, dozens of bedrooms for the singers and orchestra, and a dining hall as big and fancy as any restaurant.

It was also echoingly loud. Dozens of musicians clustered around the tables, enjoying the breakfast buffet. While his mother laughed with a group of singers, Van hid his face in a bowl of cereal, letting their voices pummel him like sleet.

"Giovanni?" His mother's voice broke through the storm. "I lead my first master class in half an hour, and you'll be on your own for the day. There's a library in the mansion that you are welcome to use, and a game room with a pool table and puzzles. And of course you can go back to our suite. You know the way."

Van nodded, half listening. His mother put a hand on his arm.

"Don't go swimming without me," his mother continued. "There's no lifeguard on duty. And, Giovanni, do *not* leave the grounds. One of the singers was just telling me about a little boy who got lost in the woods a few weeks ago and wasn't found for two days."

The grip on his arm tightened.

Van looked at his mother's face. She was gazing down, her bright smile eaten away to something thin and fragile, like a bit of toast crust on a plate.

"I'll be safe, Mom," he promised.

With a little start, his mother straightened. Her dazzling smile flashed back.

"Of course you will. There's so much to do right here at Fox Den, I'm sure you wouldn't want to leave anyway!" She placed a lily-scented kiss on his forehead. "See you this evening, *caro mio*."

Then she whisked away to a day of rehearsals and classes, and Van slunk out of the noisy dining room into a day that held nothing at all.

He tiptoed along the grand hallway. According to the brass plaques hung all around, the Fox Den had been the country home of a nineteenth-century robber baron. A portrait of the baron himself hung in the mansion's entry hall. Van had expected an eye patch or a billowing red scarf, but the robber baron was just a tubby old man with a mustache that looped all the way up over his ears. More brass plaques on the wall pointed the way to the library and the game room. Van followed their arrows.

The library turned out to be a square, shelf-lined room full of books that had obviously been bought to match the wallpaper instead of to be read. The game room, a bit farther down the hall, was crowded with grown-ups playing pool, using the computers, and ignoring the blaring TV.

Van backed away from the noise. He retraced his steps along the hall, ducked past the robber baron's mustache in the entryway, and slipped out the heavy front doors.

The morning outside was bright and quiet. Late-summer flowers bloomed in the gardens. Darting birds filled the sky like tossed confetti, and the woods all around rippled gently with the breeze. It should have been pretty. But the emptiness inside Van changed it, making the birds look lost and small, the sky too wide, and the forest like a dark sea, marooning him.

Van pulled his eyes to the ground. He took a breath. He stepped onto the forking path.

And that was when he saw it.

A few steps to his right, something pale thrust up

from the mulch beneath a blooming rosebush.

Van hesitated. He'd been heading left, toward their suite, not to the right. But his feet had already swiveled him around. In six steps, they had carried him straight to the rosebush. Van crouched beside it.

Buried in the mulch was a miniature castle.

Van pried it out of the dirt. The castle was made of pale stone, with parapets and turrets and minuscule oval windows. From its size, it might have come from an aquarium for teeny, regal fish.

The familiar thrill of found treasure prickled through him. It was nothing compared to the thrill of padding down the stone staircase into the Collection, but it was something. Slipping the castle into his pocket made the emptiness inside him seem a tiny bit less empty too.

As Van straightened up again, something else caught his eyes. Something lying in the grass a few yards down the slope. Something that glittered.

Van crept toward it. The thing was a paler shade of green than the grass around it, but if it hadn't been for that pearly glitter, he might not have spotted it at all. Van dropped to his knees in the grass.

Before him lay a green jade dragon.

He lifted it gently. The dragon had a curving tail and

claws and long, feathery whiskers. It was surprisingly heavy for something so delicate.

Van rocked back on his heels, holding the treasure. He might not be able to keep such a potentially valuable thing for himself, at least not without making sure that no one had reported it lost. But for now, he would keep it safe. Slipping the dragon into his other pocket, he rose to his feet.

He'd already moved farther down the path than he'd realized. Behind him, the mansion had dwindled into the distance. Just ahead stood the grand stone arch carved with the words FOX DEN OPERA. And beyond that arch lay the road, narrow, shady, and deserted. Van had never seen a road so quiet that it didn't even have lanes. When he kept still, listening, he couldn't hear a single car. How far would he have to follow that road before he found another person?

The thought made him shiver.

For the third time, Van started to turn back. But also for the third time, something stopped him.

Just beyond the Fox Den archway, at the side of the road, there stood a tree with a large knothole. And inside that knothole, something glimmered.

Van hesitated.

Taking just a few steps outside the grounds wasn't really breaking his promise, was it? He wasn't going to get lost, not with the road right there and Fox Den beside him. And he couldn't leave the glimmering thing there without even knowing what it was.

Van darted through the arch.

The knothole was at Van's eye level, too low for most people to see inside, deep and dark enough to hide its contents from anyone else. Cautiously, he reached inside, and drew out a heavy glass paperweight.

The air in Van's lungs turned to ice.

For a moment, he couldn't breathe. He could only stare down at the glass circle in his hand, the whorls of color trapped inside it like frozen fireworks.

He'd seen paperweights like this before.

In Mr. Falborg's collection.

Van spun in a circle. The road was deserted. There was no one in the shadows, or hiding in the rustling woods nearby. Not as far as he could see.

Could this be a coincidence? Was a glass paperweight just the sort of thing that ended up in a tree outside a fancy opera festival?

Or was someone sending him a message?

Van scanned the road once more. This time, amid

the shadows flickering over the pavement, he spotted something.

Something small and gleaming and familiar.

A penny.

Beyond that first penny, half hidden in the moss on the road's shoulder, was another penny. And another.

This wasn't a coincidence.

An icy, electric sensation, like scraping your fingernails across a frosty window, raced over Van's skin.

He raced down the shadowy road.

The pennies were scattered widely but evenly along the shoulder. Van kept his head down, picking up each coin as he found it, his eyes combing the ground for more. He spotted other small things: mushrooms as pale as pearls, ruffled fungi on rotted trunks, the thick green lace of ferns. The stash of pennies in his pocket grew heavier. Van's breaths came quicker. He was so focused on the small things below him, he didn't notice the larger things appearing all around.

He didn't notice the high brick wall looming through the woods beside him. He didn't notice the open gate in that wall, its tall iron bars topped with forbidding spikes. He didn't notice the shady lawn beyond the gate, or the building waiting at the end of it.

When the road beneath him forked, one branch leading onward into the woods, the other becoming an older, pebbled drive that wound through an open gate, Van barely paused. He had to follow the pennies. And they were leading him to the right, up that old, pebbled drive.

And then, halfway up the drive, beside a knot of evergreen trees, the trail of pennies stopped.

Van scanned the ground. He dropped to a crouch, examining the trees' roots, even looking up into their branches. There were no more pennies to be found. But behind the trees, cupped in a patch of moss, was something else.

A marble.

Van picked it up with shaking fingers.

It was made of clear glass, with a spiral of pale colors twisting inside. It made him think of a distant, mysterious planet.

It made him think of Pebble.

This wasn't the marble he'd given her—that marble was in his own pocket at this very second. But it was similar enough to freeze him in place. It was similar enough to mean something.

Behind the evergreens, a twig cracked. Footsteps shushed across the grass.

Van didn't hear this.

But he did hear the voice that came a second later.

"Well," it said. "It took you long enough."

8
Pebble

Van whipped around.

A girl stood on the path behind him.

Instead of a too-big coat full of bulging pockets, she wore a pale green shirt and spotless jeans. There was no squirrel perched on her shoulder. But she had the same sloppy ponytail, and the same ears sticking out through her thick brown hair, and the eyes, just the color of mossy pennies, of somebody he used to know.

Pebble held out one hand, palm up. "I'll need that stuff back."

Joy and shock and confusion smashed together in Van's chest. His frozen lungs tried to pull in a breath. At the same moment, several words tried to shove their way out of his mouth. Van had been on underground trains at rush hour, when masses of people tried to squeeze out the train doors while more masses of people tried to push their way in. This seemed very much like what was happening inside him right now.

He made a glugging, choking sound, something like *"Huhyuhhk?"*

"I'll need that stuff back," Pebble repeated.

Van swallowed. "You . . ." His voice wobbled so hard that he had to start over. "What do you mean, it took me long enough?"

"After I sent the postcard." Pebble flung one arm toward the top of the sloping drive. "It took you forever to get here!"

Van followed the line of Pebble's arm.

At the end of the drive, nestled against the forest, was a house. At least, Van assumed it was a house, although it looked more like a mishmash of a college and a castle. It was a rambling brick manor, with wings jutting out on each side, and tall, narrow windows, and a high tower at one end. It was a house Van had seen, sketched in ink, on the front of a battered postcard.

"Wish you were here," Van breathed. *"You* wrote that postcard? You—you wanted me to *wish* I was here?"

"Of course," said Pebble proudly. "I knew you'd figure

it out! When I came up with the plan, I couldn't believe how perfect it was." Her words came faster, beginning to blur together. "Knew *I* couldn't just wish you here, cause . . . *that* big . . . even noticed. Then . . . of a postcard, except the message couldn't be suspicious . . . thought of the *perfect* thing, and wished for it to reach you without *anybody else ever seeing it*. And it worked!" Pebble threw out her hands, looking extremely pleased with herself.

Van's mind reeled.

Pebble was here. She wasn't tied up in a tower, or locked in a golden cage like a cockatoo. She had orchestrated all of this.

"You used a wish?" Van asked shakily.

"I normally wouldn't. You know that," Pebble answered. "But I *had* to get a message to you. We barely have time to—"

"But I only found the postcard because it was stuck in a hedge," Van interrupted. "And I jumped through that hedge *because a garbage truck almost squished me*."

Pebble's eyes widened. Her mouth closed.

For a moment, the two of them stared at each other. Van couldn't be sure what Pebble was thinking, but her face seemed to be wrestling with itself. Meanwhile, Van was realizing that the garbage truck might not have been an attempted murder at all. It might have been a wish gone wrong: less cruel, but just as dangerous. He wasn't sure if that was better or worse.

"Well," said Pebble at last. "It *didn't* hit you. You're here. You wouldn't have found the card without the truck *almost* squishing you. So everything worked out. Come on," she added, straightening her shoulders. "There's a *lot* to tell you, and I have to put all of Uncle Ivor's things where they belong before he comes back."

"You mean he'll be here *soon*?" Van staggered backward. "But . . . even if the truck wasn't his fault—he still tried to kill me!"

Pebble stared at Van as though he'd started speaking in dolphin sounds. "What?"

"He wished me in front of an underground train!" Van exclaimed.

Pebble's dubious expression flickered. "Well . . . that wish must have gone wrong too," she said at last. "Uncle Ivor would never have tried to *kill* you. He just wanted you out of the way."

Nail's warning—*"She may have realigned with her uncle. She may be working with him against us"*—flared through Van's mind.

Pebble held out a hand again. "You can keep the pennies, but I need everything else back. Hurry."

With jittery fingers, Van dug into his pockets for the castle, jade dragon, paperweight, and two marbles, and dropped them all into Pebble's palm. Immediately, he wished he could snatch one marble back. He hadn't meant to hand over both of them. He'd planned to keep the older one, the one he'd given to her months ago, until he knew whether this was the same Pebble he'd given it to in the first place. But it was too late now.

Pebble's eyes went straight to the second marble. Then they locked on Van's. "I knew you'd find that too," she said. "I knew you'd keep looking." A little spark flared inside her eyes, like a match touching the wick of a birthday candle. "I knew you'd understand everything. You're the only one who would."

Then, for the first time since he'd arrived, Pebble gave him a smile.

It was like the flash of a camera, there and gone so fast that it made Van dizzy. The entire world seemed dimmer without it.

Pebble whirled away. "Come on," she called over her shoulder, her voice sharp and serious again. "We can talk inside!"

Van hung back for as long as he could stand it. Then he took off after Pebble, running hard to catch up.

The vast brick house seemed to grow as they approached. More and more wings slid into sight, more rooms and nooks and tall windows thrust out in all directions, as though the place were adding to itself before Van's eyes. By the time they stepped through its massive front door, he felt disoriented and very small.

They entered a long, high-ceilinged chamber. Three chandeliers dripping with crystals dangled from the rafters. Curio cabinets and gilt-framed oil paintings covered the wood-paneled walls. The space was so still and so solid, Van could hear the echo of his own footsteps.

"Mr. Falborg owns this place?" Van whispered.

". . . Owns a bunch of houses. He collects *them* too." Pebble turned to face Van. "You don't have to be quiet. Uncle Ivor's at an auction, and Hans and Gerda are running errands. Come this way."

She beckoned Van into the next chamber, a gigantic living room where dozens of Tiffany lamps tinged the air with light of every color. It was like being inside a kaleidoscope, Van thought. A kaleidoscope with velvet couches. And a giant fireplace. And a row of suits of armor.

"Are those real?" he said, still whispering.

"Well, they're not real *knights*. But they're real armor." Pebble unlatched a glass case in one corner and placed the jade dragon in an empty spot. "And I told you, you don't have to whisper."

But Van wasn't sure he could stop. He wasn't sure he could trust this place, or this clean, coatless Pebble, or the colliding feelings in his heart.

Pebble led the way through a hall lined with model ships, and then dashed up a staircase and into another corridor, this one filled with dangling silk and paper kites.

"Did Mr. Falborg wish all of this here from his house in the city?" Van asked, swatting a kite tail out of his face.

"Some of it," Pebble answered, opening a door to yet another staircase. ". . . collections all over the place. But he brings his most valuable things wherever he goes."

"Then—are the Wish Eaters here right now?" Van looked over his shoulder, as though he might find a few of the misty little beings floating in the air behind him.

"They're here," said Pebble shortly. "And they're secure."

"What about the ones . . ." Van remembered the

silvery, long-toothed beasts lurking in Mr. Falborg's city garden and couldn't repress a shiver. "What about the ones that weren't *little* anymore?"

Pebble threw him a look. "It's a big house."

She opened a thick wooden door.

Van trailed her across the threshold. The room inside was spacious but cozy, lit by red glass lamps hanging from the rafters and clustered with small tables. Armchairs and cushioned seats and pillowed couches waited for someone to flop onto them. The walls were lined with shelves of boxes, flat and thick, small and huge, in every color of the rainbow. Van focused on one colorful row. Candy Land. Hungry Hungry Hippos. Ten editions of Clue. Twenty versions of Monopoly.

"This is the game room," Pebble explained, placing the miniature castle on a table where the rest of a chess set waited for it. "It's probably my favorite room in this house. But it's a lot less fun when—you know." She looked away, mumbling the last few words. "What injures you."

When it's just you.

Van stepped toward an old-fashioned card catalog. He tugged open a drawer. It was filled with packs of red playing cards, all of them carefully boxed and filed away. The next drawer held green boxes. The third held pale blue.

Something in his chest began to burn.

He'd been so sure that Pebble needed him. That she was trapped somewhere, alone and miserable—as alone and miserable as she'd left him.

But she'd been *here* all along. Here, in a big country mansion full of kites and suits of armor and more games than Van had ever seen in his life.

Maybe it was the coziness of the room. Maybe it was the endless packs of cards. Maybe it was the Hungry Hungry Hippos that did it. Whatever the reason, the thing in Van's chest suddenly went *hiss—spark—FWOOSH.*

He wheeled on Pebble. "So *this* is where you've been?" he demanded. "Living in a giant mansion with every game in the world? *This* is what you've been doing while I thought you were being held prisoner?"

Pebble's mouth fell open.

But Van rushed on before she could speak. "All this time, I've been thinking, *Poor Pebble!* Or should I call you *Mabel?*"

Pebble's mouth slammed shut again. "No," she said through clenched teeth. "You shouldn't."

"Why? Isn't that your real name?" Van plowed on. "That's what Mr. Falborg calls you. Have you just been pretending to be somebody else all along? Somebody named Pebble, who lived in a secret world underground? Is that why I shouldn't call you *Mabel*, Mabel?"

"No," said Pebble tightly. "It's because if you do, I'll roll you up and stuff you inside that card catalog."

"Oh *no*. I'll be stuck forever in a big fancy room full of games. How *terrible*." Van wasn't used to being sarcastic, but he realized that he kind of liked it. It was like putting on a leather jacket that he knew wasn't his style, but that made him feel like a much tougher guy. "Does your uncle have a room full of a million Legos too? Or maybe a special collection of every kind of candy that's ever been made?"

"No," Pebble retorted. "He doesn't collect anything *edible*. It *degrades*." Her voice shrank to a murmur. "But Legos . . . yes."

"Of course he does." Van hands balled into fists. "So while everybody was terrified for you, and the Collectors were asking *me* how to find you, and I was almost getting killed by trains and garbage trucks, you were just . . . here? Playing games? Making *wishes*?"

Van shook his head so hard it made him dizzy. "Now you're making excuses for your uncle, and—"

"I'm not making excuses!" Pebble cut him off at last. "*Reasons* aren't excuses!"

"So *what are the REASONS*?" Van exploded. "Why? Why would you go with Mr. Falborg? Do you know how much I . . . how much Barnavelt has missed you?" Van's heart slammed painfully against his ribs. "How could you just *leave us*?"

The look on Pebble's face abruptly changed. Its hard expression broke like a crust of ice on cold water, and Van saw something else, something softer and sadder, underneath. Before he could get a good look at it, Pebble lunged forward and wrapped him in a tight hug.

"I missed you too," she said, close to his ear.

She broke away again, so suddenly that Van teetered. He plopped back into a red velvet armchair. It had all happened too fast for him to decide whether to hug her back. Pebble leaned low over Van's seat.

"I never said I was a prisoner," she murmured. Her mossy eyes tunneled into his. "I'm a *spy*."

Van was too dizzy to manage more than "Huh?"

Pebble locked her hands around the arms of Van's

chair and craned closer. "Why do you think I went with Uncle Ivor in the first place?"

"Because . . ." Van thought back to that terrible night. He remembered the chaos he'd caused by releasing the Eaters. He remembered Pebble saving him, helping him to escape from Jack and the other furious guards. He remembered the sparkle of Mr. Falborg's backyard fountain, the monstrous Wish Eaters lurking in the trees, the coin with Mr. Falborg's wish arcing through the dim night air. He remembered Pebble stepping into Mr. Falborg's open arms, leaving Van and Barnavelt behind. "Because he wished for you to join him. And deep down, you must have wanted to."

Pebble shook her head hard. "I still care about Uncle Ivor. But that doesn't mean I think he's *right*." She stared into Van's eyes. "I knew that I could use this chance to watch him. I could find out how he kept his Wish Eaters, and about what he was planning to do next. And *then* I could reach out to *you*."

Van studied Pebble's face. He often learned more from people's eyes than from the words that came out of their mouths. And Pebble's eyes were wide. Intent. Desperate for him to believe.

"I wasn't leaving the Collectors," she went on.

"Not for good. That's why I hid those clues at Uncle Ivor's house, so you'd know I was still on your side. But I had to be careful, to make sure Uncle Ivor never suspected, or all of this would be *pointless*. I just had to wait and hope that you understood. And that you hadn't just . . . just forgotten about me."

Pebble stopped, breathing hard.

"Nobody forgot about you," said Van.

Pebble took her hands off the arms of his chair. She pushed herself upright, looking away and blinking rapidly. Van wasn't sure, but he thought he even saw her sniffle.

"So," she said, meeting Van's eyes again. "Do you believe me?"

Van took a turn keeping quiet.

This Pebble had made wishes. Dangerous wishes. This Pebble was defending Ivor Falborg, who may or may not have tried to murder Van with a wish and a train. This Pebble looked and even *smelled* different from the girl he remembered. The girl he'd trusted with his life.

"I *want* to believe you," he said at last.

Pebble nodded. Her shoulders rose and fell with a deep breath. "Then I have something to show you."

9
Wishing Well

They left the house by a back door.

Pebble charged across a narrow back lawn and into the woods, with Van jogging after her. Van had never set foot in these woods before, and yet, all of this felt oddly familiar. How many times had he let Pebble lead him into something he didn't understand? He'd chased her across city parks, up water towers, through underground passageways. If he made his eyes unfocus, he could almost see her old bulky coat flapping behind her, the puff of a silvery tail hanging over her shoulder. Van's heart ached.

"I wish—" he said aloud.

Pebble stopped so suddenly that Van smacked into her.

"What are you doing?" she asked, wide-eyed. "Are you *wishing*?"

"No, I . . . I just . . . ," Van stammered. "Not a *real* wish. I don't have anything to wish on, anyway."

"Oh." Pebble's shoulders relaxed slightly. "I thought you might . . ." She looked down at Van's empty hands. "Never mind."

"Would it even matter if I did make a wish?" Van asked. "I thought Wish Eaters usually stay in towns and cities. Except for the ones in your uncle's house, anyway. Are there even any Wish Eaters out here?"

Pebble gave Van a brief, needle-sharp look. "Eaters do keep to towns," she said, turning back to the woods. "Most of the time."

They were only a few yards into the trees, but the forest was so thick that the vast brick house had already disappeared. The bracken around them was dense and green. Pebble plunged through it, hopping over fallen logs and dodging thorny bushes. Her ponytail waved behind her like a flag.

She glanced back, saying something Van couldn't catch. "What . . . issue . . . ?"

"What did you say?" Van asked.

Pebble turned her head a bit farther but didn't

slow down. "What were you going to wish for?"

"Oh." Van stumbled over a mossy fallen trunk. "I just thought it would be nice if Barnavelt was here."

For a moment, Pebble didn't speak. Van couldn't catch sight of her face, but he saw her shoulders fall, as though something heavy had settled there. . . . *wish seer too,* he thought he heard her murmur.

That was something he'd missed about Pebble, Van realized. Her big eyes, the shape of her mouth, and her posture told him so much. Even when he couldn't catch what she said, it was easy to understand what she felt.

It was easy for someone who bothered to look, anyway.

They threaded through the trees, snapping twigs beneath their shoes. Cool wind gusted around them. Each fresh breeze set off a wave of rustling, shivering, swaying motions that hit Van from all sides, like a flood threatening to close over his head. It made Van catch his breath.

He didn't like this: being surrounded by unpredictable movement, never knowing which way to look. He missed being in the city, where at least the walls around you stood still.

They walked for what felt to Van like miles, until at

last they reached a patch of forest where the trees grew sparser and larger. Giant oaks towered around them. Breaking through the moss beneath their feet, Van spotted the line of a well-worn path.

Pebble slowed her steps at last.

"Good," she said, turning back toward Van. "No one's here."

Then she bolted down the path, with Van running behind her.

They stumbled out into a clearing.

Van stared around. The clearing was wide enough that the leafy canopy unraveled above them, allowing slips of sunlight to tumble through. The ground was soft with moss. At the clearing's center, a pool of fallen leaves surrounded something made of wood and stone. At first glance, Van thought it was a tiny house—someplace just the right size for raccoons, or possibly trolls. But as he edged nearer, he saw that it was something else entirely.

It was an ancient well.

Its stone walls formed an uneven circle. Its shingled roof sagged, covered in moss and tiny mushrooms. A broken wooden handle stuck out from its side, although there was no rope and no bucket.

"Was this what you wanted to show me?" Van asked. "An old well?" He craned cautiously over its stone wall. The well was too deep for him to see its bottom. It made him think of the Collection, its pit plunging down, down, down into the dark. Only here, from somewhere far below, he caught the faintest silvery twinkle. "Is there even any water in here?"

Pebble stepped close to him.

"It's not just a well," she said. "It's a *wishing* well."

Van looked from Pebble's mossy-penny eyes back to the twinkling depths. "So people wish on coins and throw them down here?"

"Exactly."

Van glanced at the shadowy woods, the thousands of trees swaying between the two of them and anyone else. "*What* people?"

"This well has been here for hundreds of years. Uncle Ivor's been researching it. A long, long time ago, a little village was built right here, in the woods. Eventually all the people moved away. But some of them remembered the well and would come here to make wishes. Some people still come, following the paths through the woods."

Van touched the lip of the well. The stones were cool

and damp, as though the earth was exhaling straight through it. He pictured centuries' worth of coins piling up down there in the watery dark.

"What happens to the wishes?" he asked. "I mean, if there are no Collectors or Wish Eaters around here . . ."

"There *are*," said Pebble.

"Okay. *One* Collector." Van nodded at Pebble. "Is *that* what you're doing here? You're going to collect all the old wishes? Does that even work?"

"No." Pebble shook her head sharply. She leaned even closer to Van, so he could feel as well as hear her voice on his skin. "One *Eater*."

A blossom of frost filled Van's stomach.

He could almost feel little Lemmy, misty and cool and practically weightless, curling up in his hands. And at the same time, he could hear the roar of the monstrous Eaters in the Hold, with their alligator jaws and their staring white eyes.

"Down at the bottom of that well," Pebble went on, "is the biggest, oldest, strongest Wish Eater left in this half of the world."

The frost in Van's stomach spread. A chill prickled down his legs and up into the roots of his hair.

"It's stayed hidden down there, feeding on the

wishes people give it, for hundreds of years." Pebble's eyes were wide. "And it's probably been alive a lot longer than that."

"It's right down there?" Van whispered. He squinted uneasily at the glittering dark. "Can it hear us?"

"And smell us," Pebble murmured back. "And feel us."

For a beat, they both kept silent. Van pictured the beast stretched out far below them, a massive body winding through the cold dirt like the roots of an invisible tree.

A tremor traveled up through the soles of his shoes.

"Did you feel that?" he asked.

Pebble blinked. "Feel what?"

"*That.* Something under us."

Pebble shook her head. "I don't feel anything."

But something underground had stirred. Van was certain. The slow, shifting motions trembled up through the earth, straight through the spot where he stood. It wasn't a pleasant feeling. It was a little like standing on a grave and feeling the soil beneath your feet start to move.

Pebble grasped him by the arm. In a few quick steps, she'd dragged him out of the clearing, back into the cover of the trees.

"*That* is why we're here right now." She faced him head-on, speaking in a louder, quicker voice. "That's why Uncle Ivor bought that house to begin with. He's been buying up the woodland all around it. A few weeks ago, he bought *this* spot too."

Van stared into Pebble's eyes. "What's he going to do?"

"He's playing too close to the well," she answered. As she rushed on, explaining about finding Uncle Ivor's building plans, and about construction starting next week, Van realized he'd misheard. *He's planning to enclose the well.*

"He's pretending that he's starting a spring water bottling company," said Pebble. "But really, he just wants the Eater."

Van glanced toward the clearing. "But Mr. Falborg already has everything anyone could want. Why does he need more?"

"Because," Pebble leaned close. "He wants the things that he *can't* have. The things he can't get just by wishing."

"Like the Eaters?"

"Like the Eaters." Pebble nodded. "Like access to the Collection. Like the dead wishes—he used to be obsessed with getting one of those. Like *me*." She paused, folding her arms tight across her chest. "Uncle Ivor isn't a *Collector*. He can't gather wishes himself. He can't control them. He can only use someone else's power." Her eyes flicked back to the clearing. "And this Eater is one of the most powerful things on earth."

Van couldn't hold back a shiver.

Pebble's sharp eyes watched him. "This is why I need your help," she went on. "We have to stop him. You have to get word to the Collectors. They need to come and trap the Eater before Uncle Ivor can take it for himself."

Van swayed, unsure if the unbalance he felt came from another movement deep underground or from something else entirely.

So Pebble *was* still a Collector. She was working against Mr. Falborg. She wanted to catch a rare and ancient being and imprison it forever.

And she needed Van's help to do it.

"You want *me* to get the message to the Collectors?" Van asked.

"That's why I wrote to you," Pebble rushed on. "You're the only one who can do it. I have no way to get to the city. And the Collection is wish-proof, so I can't reach them the way I reached you. I need you to go to them in person and tell them to get here *next Friday.* Uncle Ivor will be home all week, but he'll be busy on Friday night. He plans to start building on Saturday, so it's the only chance we have."

"Next Friday," Van repeated. He imagined the hush of the clearing demolished by the Holders' iron hooks and spiderweb nets. He imagined the Collectors driving a huge, howling creature from its home and into a tiny cell where, centuries or millennia from now, it would finally disappear for good.

An ache chewed the edge of his heart.

"If the Wish Eater has been here for centuries," he said, "hiding in its well, not hurting anyone, couldn't we just leave it there and try to stop Mr. Falborg instead?"

Pebble shook her head. "You can't stop Uncle Ivor when he wants something. That's why he does dangerous things. When he finds something he wants, it's like nothing else exists."

Van felt a twinge of recognition. He knew how it felt to spot a treasure. To have the world become a blur around you, to ignore the busy traffic and your mother calling your name as you reached out for the only thing that seemed to matter.

"Okay," he said. "But maybe we could trick him somehow. We could hide the deed to the land. Or maybe we could lead a bunch of people here on a big picnic, so when his building crew comes, they—"

But Pebble just shook her head harder. "No. He's not going to give up. As long as that Eater is down there, *everyone* is in danger."

Van stared down at Pebble's feet. Her shoes weren't the battered, squashy-looking canvas sneakers he'd always seen her wear before. These shoes were brand-new and obviously expensive, with sturdy soles and green accents on their leather sides. So much about her had changed. But underneath the clothing, so much hadn't.

Pebble touched his arm. "Van," she said. "I know you feel sorry for the Eaters. But you've seen what they can become. My uncle can't have something like this in his collection. He *can't*."

"He can't," Van agreed, very softly.

"So you'll help me?" Pebble's grip on his arm tightened. "Please?"

Van took a breath. The scents of the woods—moss and mud and pine—swirled through him. His thoughts swirled even faster. He wasn't sure what was safe, or what was kind, or what was right anymore.

"I don't even know if I'll be able to get to the city," Van hedged. "My mother took a job here for the whole season. I don't know when we'll be going back. . . ."

Pebble's hand slipped from his arm. Her body seemed to deflate, shrinking, until her eyes couldn't even meet his anymore. "I thought you were on my side," she said.

Van barely caught the words. He'd never seen Pebble look so small.

"I *am* on your side," he said, even though he wasn't sure he meant it. He just couldn't stand to see Pebble looking like that. Not when he was the only one in the world who could help her. "I'll figure it out. I'll get them the message."

Pebble's eyes flashed to his. They blazed so brightly that Van could feel himself catching fire too. "I knew you would," she said.

She straightened up, her shoulders falling, her spine unbending. "We'd better get back." Before Van could speak again, she had whirled away.

Van raced into the trees behind her. He kept his eyes fixed on her ponytail as they ran, trying to shove the sense of that presence underneath the well down into the deepest, darkest corner of his mind.

10
Through the Woods

"Mom?"

Van's mother glanced up from the musical score spread out on the piano rack. "Yes, *caro mio*?"

Van slid off the couch and sidled closer. He'd been waiting for the perfect moment to broach the subject, which had meant not rushing to find his mother until she was done with the day's rehearsals, keeping quiet all through dinner with the directors, and strolling patiently back to their suite as though he didn't have a question waiting to burst out of him like a cat being released from a kitty carrier.

Now everything was calm. He would have his mother's full attention.

Or eighty percent of it, anyway.

"You said we could go back to the city whenever we need to, right?" Van asked.

"That's right!" His mother circled a run of notes with her pencil. "We're just a pleasant train ride away. Aren't we lucky?"

"Then . . . could we go back tomorrow?"

"Tomorrow!" His mother laughed. "We just got here!"

"I know, but . . . I need something."

His mother's eyebrows rose slightly. "What do you need?"

Van leafed through a pile of mental options. Clothes? She'd never believe it. A book? She'd say it could wait, or tell him to look for one in the mansion library. Medicine? Too dangerous. But maybe . . .

"I think something might be wrong with my hearing aids," said Van.

His mother's eyebrows folded into a frown. "Really?" She pulled Van closer to the piano bench, examining his ears as though she might be able to see a broken piece in the tiny machines. "I'll call the audiologist."

"No," said Van quickly. He'd chosen wrong. He'd have to back carefully out again. "I probably just need to change the batteries."

"And we brought plenty of those," said his mother. "Try that, and let me know if it doesn't get better." She turned back toward the score, lightly touching a trio of keys.

The sounds of the piano bumped Van's thoughts out of order. He chewed on his lower lip. "So when do you think we *will* go back to the city?"

His mother tilted her head, playing another ripple of notes. "Probably two . . . maybe three weeks."

"Weeks?" Van burst out.

"Yes." His mother glanced at him, eyebrows raised again. "There's so much to do here, getting ready for the first production. *Hansel and Gretel* opens in just over a week. After that, you'll start meeting with your tutor, and soon you'll be just as busy as I am!"

"But . . ." Desperation pushed Van into unexpected places. "I really—kind of—miss Peter."

Now his mother took both hands off the keyboard. She turned to him, eyebrows rising even higher. "Peter *Grey*?" she said, as though Van might have meant Peter Pan, or Peter Peter Pumpkin Eater.

"Yes," said Van. "We had plans. To do some fun things together." Mixing a few true ingredients into the lie couldn't hurt. "But we left so suddenly, Peter and I didn't get the chance to do any of them."

"Oh," said his mother. "Giovanni . . . I'm sorry." She touched his cheek. "My work makes some things harder for both of us. Lots of new adventures, fewer old friends." She gave him a gentle smile. "In three weeks, I promise, we'll head back to the city, and you can have a nice long visit with Peter."

"Three weeks," Van repeated.

"I just can't get away from my work any earlier than that." His mother's hand left his cheek. "Thank you for understanding, *caro mio.*"

She turned back to the music. A moment later, the sounds of the piano filled the room.

The notes crowded Van's head. He bolted to his bedroom, taking out his hearing aids and dropping them on the bedside table.

Three weeks.

He couldn't wait three weeks.

By that time, Mr. Falborg would have enclosed the wishing well and trapped the Wish Eater. By that time, Van would have failed Pebble and everyone else.

He sagged to his knees in front of his miniature stage. SuperVan still posed there. Alone.

"Hey!" called an imaginary voice. "SuperVan!"

SuperVan seemed to stand a bit taller. "Who is that?"

"SuperVan!" the voice called. It was coming from within Van's treasure box. "SuperVan, help me! I need you!"

Van nudged SuperVan toward the sound. "Pawn Girl? Is that you?"

"Yes, it's me!" Van imagined the wooden pawn calling back. "I'm trapped inside the White Wizard's fortress!"

SuperVan's plastic feet remained on the stage floor. "I can't move! Something has stolen my power of flight!"

"But—but you're *SuperVan*." Pawn Girl sounded brokenhearted. "Isn't there any way to get your powers back?"

Van thought.

Maybe there was a way.

He glanced through the bedroom window. The woods had turned silver gray in the twilight, the treetops stretching away as far as he could see. But when Van got up and pressed his forehead to the glass, he thought he could just make out the peaked roof of a tall brick tower, far away. And beyond that, Van knew, somewhere deep in the silver-gray shadows, was the wishing well.

In his mind, the seed of a plan began to grow.

* * *

Late that night, after his mother had come in to give him a kiss and settled down to sleep in her own bedroom, Van sat up in bed. He'd kept his clothes on under the covers. Fitting his hearing aids into his ears and his feet into his shoes, he crept out of their suite into the night.

The grounds were deserted. Up the winding paths ahead of him, the Fox Den mansion twinkled with dim lights. A half moon illuminated the sleeping outbuildings, the quiet gardens, and rippling koi ponds. With a last glance over his shoulder, Van dashed across the grass and into the woods.

The pennies he'd gathered on the road knocked together in his pocket. As Van hurried through the thickening trees, their weight thumped against his leg, seeming to grow heavier and heavier. But he wasn't going to slow down. And he wasn't going to change his mind. He had promised Pebble his help, and there was only one way he could think of to keep that promise.

He would have to use a wish.

Van understood the dangers. A wish had hurt his mother. A wish had forced him to help damage the Collection. A wish had nearly squashed him—twice.

But wishes had also gotten Van safely from place to place. They had let him help his friends. Once, when Van had plummeted from the top of a city building, a wish had even saved his life. He reminded himself of those good wishes as he rushed along.

Besides, the danger of Mr. Falborg claiming the ancient Eater was far greater than the danger in any single wish.

All Van had to do was find his way back to the wishing well.

Fortunately, finding his way through strange places was one of Van's greatest talents. He'd been his mother's navigator in every city they'd visited since he was five years old. Because Van noticed details—an unusual door, a striped awning, a grumpy-faced cat glowering at them through a window—he could walk a route just once and remember it. He would retrace his steps by following the chain of images: cat, awning, unusual door.

But as Van raced deeper into the woods, he discovered something.

The woods didn't have doors. Or awnings. Or grumpy cats behind glass.

The woods had trees. That was all. And in the darkness, all trees looked the same. They were a crush of silhouettes, black on gray on black. They closed around him like jagged fences, or like the rungs of a giant, crooked cage.

Van glanced over his shoulder. The glow from the Fox Den had vanished. The air below the canopy was blue black. Branches and brush tangled around him.

If he turned around now, he might be able to find his way back to the Fox Den's lights. Or he might not. He might become even more disoriented, with even less time. And he'd be even further from keeping his promise.

There was nothing to do but press on.

Van took a breath, aimed his feet at the spot where the wishing well should be, and ran.

There was no wind. The woods were still. But every now and then, a burst of motion—a thrashing branch where an animal had bolted out of Van's path, or a flash of moonlight on dark wings—would snag his eye, and fear would trip him, like the tree roots breaking through the forest floor.

He kept his eyes sharp for the lights of the Falborg mansion. It was the one marker he could count on recognizing. Once he passed it, he'd know that he was on the right course. He'd been running for long enough that he had to be getting close by now.

But there was no sign of the trees thinning. And there were no lights.

No lights at all.

Once again, Van halted.

He spun in a quick circle.

There were no lights *anywhere*.

No houses. No streetlights. Even the moon had vanished behind a velvet curtain of clouds.

Van stood, breathing hard. The forest loomed around him. He tried to reorient himself, but with no landmarks and no light, he couldn't be sure which direction was which.

He was still wavering there when, among the shadows just over his shoulder, he caught the flicker of something moving closer.

Van broke into a run once more.

It was probably just a raccoon, he told himself as he pelted through the trees. *Maybe a deer.* Something harmless and furry and just as startled by Van as Van was by it. But his body didn't listen. It hurtled onward, through the shadows.

Van glanced back again. He couldn't see the thing that had startled him, but he could sense it, still there, still close. He could feel its eyes.

Maybe it was following him.

Maybe it was something furry and startled but not so harmless. Were there wolves in these woods? Or bears? Or something worse?

In a burst of panic, Van ran even faster. Tree bark scraped his arms. Twigs ripped at his hair. The canopy thickened, and Van was sealed in the darkness beneath it, alone with his ragged breathing and thundering heart, and with whatever was chasing him. Out of the corner of his eye, too deep in the shadows for him to see clearly, the undergrowth rippled where something big had rushed through.

The thing was *definitely* following him.

Van ran faster still. He ran until his legs and lungs and his head ached. He ran as fast as he had ever run, but he couldn't get away from the truth.

He was lost. There was no sign of the Falborg house. No sign of the path to the well. No sign of anything familiar. There was only the surrounding darkness, and the thing that was hidden by it.

Without slowing, Van fumbled in his pockets. He hadn't thought to bring anything useful: a knife or a compass or even a flashlight. All he had was the stash of pennies. He should have left a trail of coins to follow back home. But it was too late now.

Much too late.

A few feet to his right, a patch of leaves fluttered. Whatever was hunting him had drawn closer. Van thought of his mother, squeezing his arm and telling him not to wander in the woods. He thought of Pebble, begging him for help. He thought of the promises he'd made. With a last surge of speed, he charged forward, crashed through a knot of vines, and sprawled over a fallen tree onto a patch of dewy grass.

Grass?

Gasping, Van scrambled to his feet. Had he somehow reached the clearing after all?

He looked around.

The Fox Den mansion stood a hundred yards away.

Van was gazing up at the back of it, the side with fountained ponds and lush green gardens. A few outdoor lights glowed steadily. Beyond the mansion, the grounds and outbuildings slept beneath the cloudy sky.

He had run in a giant loop and ended up back where he'd begun.

Van whirled around.

The woods behind him were still. Whatever had been following him was nowhere to be seen. It must have backed away from the lights, keeping hidden within the trees . . . unless he had imagined it completely.

No, Van told himself. He had felt the air stirring behind him. He could still catch the prickling sensation of eyes watching him, peering out from the darkness.

Maybe.

Van swayed on the grass, taking deep breaths. The forest remained perfectly still. He should have been relieved—and he *was*—but he was also no closer to helping Pebble. And he wouldn't get any closer tonight.

Finally, exhausted and aching, Van turned and stumbled toward the gardens.

He shuffled along the paved paths. Scents of roses and pond water draped the air around him like invisible lace curtains. At the edge of one stone pond, Van slowed, watching droplets fall from its marble fountain and ripple the black water below.

He'd met Pebble beside a city park fountain. He'd lost her next to another fountain, in Mr. Falborg's backyard. Now he'd found her again . . . but everything had changed. Now both he and Pebble were stuck in that gray place between enemy sides, without anyone to help them.

Except each other.

Van reached into his pocket. The pennies felt warm

and solid in his hand. He pulled one out and held it on his palm, letting it wink darkly in the moonlight. He thought of all the wishes he'd made before he'd even known about Collectors or Eaters. There must have been hundreds of them—wishes made on eyelashes and coins and ladybugs, wishes on birthday candles and stars. Maybe, Van thought, the wishes you made without the hope of help from magical creatures were just wishes you had to make come true for yourself.

So Van wished.

I wish I could find a way to help Pebble.

The dark dot of the penny hit the water, making one more ripple.

Van straightened his shoulders. He turned away from the fountain, wound through the gardens to the front of the mansion, and padded down the path to the old stables. A moment later, he was shut inside of his suite, and the Fox Den lay silent beneath the moon-gray sky.

Another minute slipped by.

From the edge of the woods, something crept out into the moonlight.

The thing was pale and four-legged, formed like an animal—but not like any animal that belonged in those woods. Its large body drifted over the grass as lightly as a trail of fog. Its eyes took in everything: the sleeping mansion, the dark gardens, the glimmer of water in the pools.

The thing floated through the gardens. It stopped beside a stone fountain. One long-fingered hand clawed through the pool, catching a small, golden light.

The thing swallowed the light.

Silvery mist filled the air. Its shimmer blanketed the rose beds and swirled along the paved paths. Before the mist had thinned once more, the thing was gone.

And the phone beside Ingrid Markson's bed began to buzz.

11
Doom Will Get You Anyway

By the time Van woke, the midmorning sun was pouring its gold light through his window.

"Good morning, sleepyhead!" sang his mother when Van stumbled out into the hall. She swiveled in her seat at the kitchen table, her smile dimming slightly as her eyes fell on Van. "Are you all right, *caro mio*? You look like you slept in your clothes!"

"Oh. Um . . ." Van glanced down at his wrinkled and mud-dabbled pants. "I guess I did. I was really tired."

"Yes, you dozed right through the coaching sessions I held here in the living room this morning." His mother took a sip of her tea. "Now I don't have any other obligations until tomorrow afternoon. Instead, I have a special surprise for you." Her smile returned to room-bleaching wattage. "Charles and Peter Grey will be here in less than an hour!"

Van felt as though both his knees had disappeared. He swayed, managing to catch himself against the wall. Maybe he had misheard; he hadn't put in his hearing aids yet. Maybe his mother had said something else. Something less horrible.

"They what?" he croaked.

"After our talk yesterday evening, I sent Charles a message telling him how sorry I felt about rushing you away. He wrote back late last night and said they would come up to spend the weekend with us!"

Van clutched the wall harder. "The whole weekend?"

"Well . . . one night, anyway," his mother amended. "You and Peter can have a sleepover here while Charles takes one of the guest rooms in the mansion. He and the company director are old friends." His mother's eyebrows rose. "Giovanni, aren't you happy about this? You told me you missed Peter. . . ."

"Oh. Yes. I did," Van scrambled. "I mean—I just thought we'd go to the city to see him."

"Well, the city is coming to us instead!" His mother's smile flashed back. She lifted her teacup. "Now go and shower!" she commanded over its rim. *"Andiamo!*

So you can be ready when your doom arrives!"

Van stumbled backward. "What?"

His mother set her cup down. "So you can be ready when the two of them arrive! Go on! *Andiamo!*"

Shut inside the bathroom, Van buried his head in a towel and tried to think. But all he could think about was how hard it was to solve a problem, and how easy it was to make a problem worse.

Forty-five minutes later, his doom arrived.

Van stood in the doorway, neatly dressed, his damp hair combed and his hearing aids in place. His mother glowed beside him in a pale blue blouse. And Peter, climbing out of his father's sleek black car in his expensive gray clothes, looked like a bullet coming from a gun. A very mopey bullet. A bullet that was headed straight toward Van.

Peter stopped so close to him that Van could feel his breath as he spoke. "What's going on?" he whispered, close to Van's ear. "I thought we were trying to keep them apart!"

"I—" Van began. But he was interrupted by his mother, who was giving both Greys kisses on the cheeks, and by Mr. Grey shaking his hand, and by the shattered plans wheeling around in his head.

"Are you two hungry?" Van's mother asked. "Shall we go to the dining hall?"

"We hate you for leaving," said Mr. Grey.

No. *We ate before leaving.* That made more sense. The smile Mr. Grey was giving Van's mother certainly didn't look like hate.

"Why don't we all take a walk around the grounds then?" Van's mother sang. "It's such a lovely day, and such a lovely place."

Mr. Grey offered her his arm. "And such lovely company."

Van heard those words perfectly clearly.

So, obviously, did Peter.

He hung back next to Van as Mr. Grey and Van's mother set off, glaring at their parents' backs with ice-water eyes.

"I didn't mean for this to happen," said Van to Peter, once the adults had strode out of hearing.

Peter muttered something Van couldn't catch. He stalked after their parents. Van scurried behind, wishing that his mother weren't leaning quite so heavily on Mr. Grey's arm, and that her smile didn't look quite so happy.

After their walk around the grounds, Van suggested

that they all play Monopoly in the mansion's game room. He wasn't really a Monopoly fan, but he wanted to keep all four of them together for as long as possible, so that Mr. Grey and his mother couldn't steal any more time alone.

Three hours later, Van's head was pounding from trying to separate the Greys' voices from the background noise, his mother was glassy-eyed with boredom, and Mr. Grey—who kept calling Park Place "Park Lane" in his emphatic British accent—looked wrinkled and annoyed. Only Peter was smiling.

They had dinner together in the grand dining hall. Peter asked his father to "pass the WAAAAAUUUTER" in a glass-rattling belch.

"Peter," said Mr. Grey, through tight lips.

It took Van several attempts, but he finally managed to burp out the word "cheese" loudly enough that Peter snorted water through his nose.

Dinner wrapped up pretty quickly after that.

The blue haze of twilight hung around them as Peter, Van, and Van's mother headed down the paths toward the old stables.

"Don't stay up *too* late," said Van's mother as the boys settled down in Van's room, Van on the bed and Peter on a cot borrowed from the mansion's guest rooms. His mother had loaned them the TV from her own bedroom too, so they could have a "real slumber party," as she kept saying, with a big smile.

"Good night, Peter," said Van's mother, pulling the blankets up over him. *"Buona notte, caro mio,"* she added in a softer voice, bending down to kiss Van on the forehead. The scent of lilies followed her as she swished out the door.

Van rubbed the kiss away with his sleeve, mildly embarrassed. But Peter wasn't watching. He was gazing at the door with an empty look in his blue eyes. It was a look that made Van wonder how long it had been since anyone had kissed Peter Grey good night.

They found a superhero movie on TV—the kind with enough explosions that they couldn't have heard each other even if they tried to talk. Van dozed off before it ended.

He woke up with a start a little while later, blinking around, trying to remember why he'd fallen asleep with his hearing aids still in his ears.

The TV volume had been turned low. The glow of the screen revealed Peter Grey lying on the other bed, its blue light glinting in his open eyes.

Van wouldn't be sneaking to the wishing well tonight either.

With a little sigh, he flopped back against the pillows.

Peter's eyes flicked toward him. ". . . You awake?"

"I'm awake," murmured Van. "Can't you sleep?"

Peter mumbled an answer.

Van leaned over and clicked on the small bedside lamp, illuminating Peter's face. Peter blinked in the glow.

"I can hear you better if I can see you too," Van explained.

"Oh." Peter kept still for a moment. Then, rolling his head on the pillow so that it faced Van, he said, "It's so *quiet* out here. At home, even in the middle of the night, you can hear the city." Awkwardness fluttered over his face. "I mean, not *you*. Just . . . *people* can hear the city. I mean—"

"I know what you mean," Van interrupted. "You can always feel the city too. People walking around. The traffic making the walls move." He glanced at the windows, where the black sky floated its scattering of stars. "It's harder to get to sleep out here."

". . . least it's just for one night." Peter gave his pillow a punch. "Hopefully we'll leave early tomorrow."

"If we're as bad at breakfast as we were at dinner, I bet you will." Van started to smile. "That was a pretty great burp you did. I thought your dad's wineglass was going to fall over."

Peter's grin flashed in the light. "Yours wasn't bad either."

"I'll keep practicing." Van grinned back.

They went silent again.

Van gazed at the window, trying to pull his thoughts back toward his promise to Pebble, but for some reason, his mind kept returning to the look on Peter's face when Van's mother had tucked him in.

"Do you ever miss your mom?" The words slipped out before Van could stop them.

"What?" Peter's voice was harder now. Colder.

Van shut his mouth. He shouldn't have asked. He shouldn't have said anything at all. Being quiet was always safest.

Peter kept quiet too, for so long that Van thought he wasn't going to answer at all.

But then he murmured, "I don't really remember her. She died when I was little. And she and my dad were already separated, so it wasn't like everything changed. Just half of everything."

Van lay perfectly still, taking in each word.

"Do you ever miss your dad?" Peter asked.

"I don't remember him either," said Van. "He and my mom were only together for a little while. It's always been just me and her."

Peter frowned slightly. "Do you ever get lonely? With just the two of you?"

"I didn't use to," said Van honestly. "But now I . . . I miss the city. I miss some people there." He swallowed hard. "That's actually why you're here. I told my mother I wanted to visit. But I thought we'd be going *there*, not the other way around."

"Oh," said Peter, his voice even chillier than before. "So there was somebody else who you really wanted to see."

"There's somebody I *need* to see." Van leaned into the gap between his bed and Peter's cot. "I promised that I'd help somebody. I'm supposed to get an important message to them. But now I *can't*."

"Can't you just text them or something?"

"No. I have to get the message to them in person, or . . ."

A little of the chilliness was leaving Peter's voice. "Or what?"

"I can't tell you," said Van. "I'm sorry. I really wish I could."

The word "wish" gave him a sharp, painful jolt, like he had just bitten his own tongue.

For a beat, both boys kept still.

Peter grabbed the remote and muted the TV. A sudden hush blanketed them.

"*I'm* going back to the city tomorrow," said Peter slowly.

Van met Peter's eyes. In the dimness, their icy blue color disappeared. Now they were just two bright sparks, staring back at him.

"I could take the message for you," Peter finished.

Van drew in a breath.

He wasn't sure he could trust Peter with this. He wasn't even sure if he could trust Peter not to trip him when he walked by.

But what other option did he have? He'd already lost two days, and his own plans kept crumbling under him like a floor tiled with soggy graham crackers. Soon it would be too late.

"Just a minute," he whispered.

Van slipped out of bed. He dug in his top dresser drawer until he'd found a notebook and pen, hunching over the paper so that Peter couldn't see. By the glow of the dim light, he wrote:

Dear Nail and Jack and Sesame and everyone—

This is Van Markson. I'm sending you this letter because I am far away, at Fox Den Opera, and I can't get it to you fast enough by myself. A boy I know is delivering it for me.

Pebble and Mr. Falborg are here. They have a big house nearby. There's an old wishing well in the woods, and Pebble says the Eater living in it is one of the oldest ones on earth. Mr. Falborg is going to try to trap it and keep it for himself.

You need to come here this Friday evening to stop him.

Pebble and I will be watching for you.

Please.

Van

Van underlined the final "please" three times.

He folded the paper into a little packet. He didn't have tape or staples or stickers, but in the bottom of the drawer, he found one miniature Band-Aid. Van sealed the note shut.

He turned to find Peter kneeling on the floor beside his model stage.

Peter had taken a few treasures out of the box and

arranged them next to SuperVan: a cluster of trees, a plastic bear, a tiny china squirrel.

The same tiny china squirrel that Van had stolen from Peter's own bedroom.

Van's heart shot into his windpipe.

But Peter wasn't acting suspicious. He merely moved the squirrel through the plastic trees, steering it by its quirked china tail.

"Um . . . ," said Van shakily. "Here's the message."

Peter looked up. "What do I do with it?"

"You need to take it to a place called City Collection Agency." Van's heart, still wedged in his windpipe, was pounding, making his entire body shudder slightly. "It's a little gray office between a fancy bakery and a pet store. . . ." He sketched a map on the back of the note and passed it to Peter. "Don't wait for anybody to come out. Don't even knock. Just slide the note under the door and leave."

"City Collection Agency," Peter repeated. "Do you owe somebody money or something?"

"No," said Van. "It's nothing like that."

"Really? Are you sure?" One corner of Peter's mouth tugged upward. "Van, is the mob after you?"

A surprised laugh slipped out of Van. The pounding

of his heart softened just a bit. "You'll take it there as soon as you can, right?"

"I promise." Peter slid the note and the map into his pajama pocket. He turned back toward the scene on the stage, bumping the china squirrel with one finger. "I used to have a squirrel just like this, I think."

Van's heart moved throatward again.

"Uh . . . ," he squeezed out. "It *is* yours. I took it from your room. A long time ago. During your birthday party."

"You did?" Peter stared up at Van. His eyes were wide. Not angry—just surprised.

"I'm really sorry." Van squeezed his fingernails into his palms. "I just—I wanted it so much. You should take it back."

"That's okay," said Peter lightly. "I don't need it. You can keep it."

"Really?"

"Yeah. I never used those animals anyway. It's yours now."

"Then you should take something else in exchange," said Van. He dropped onto his knees next to Peter and placed one hand on his collection box. "Something special. What do you want?"

Peter shook his head. "I don't need to take one of your treasures."

"No. Really," Van insisted. "You can pick whatever you want."

When Peter still didn't move, Van reached into the box himself. He fumbled through the layers of buttons and keychains and cake toppers and decorative erasers, until his fingers closed around something truly special.

"Here," he said, pulling it out and pressing it into Peter's palm.

Peter raised it into the glow of the bedside lamp. "What is it?"

"Amber," said Van. "I found it on a beach in Germany. And you can see that there's an ancient leaf trapped inside."

"Whoa," breathed Peter.

Even in the dim light, the amber glowed like a candle through a jar of honey. Inside its warm, gold heart sat the teardrop shape of a tiny leaf—a leaf that had fallen from some long-dead tree thousands or even millions of years ago.

Watching Peter squint down at the sparkling amber made Van think of the marble he'd pressed into Pebble's hand just after meeting her for the first time. Both

times, sharing this small, special part of himself had
felt like the right thing to do. Maybe giving a treasure
to the right person could be as exciting as finding it in
the first place.

"You're sure I can keep this?" asked Peter.

"Yes." Van smiled. "It's yours."

Peter slipped the amber carefully into his pajama
pocket, along with Van's folded note.

The boys climbed back into their beds. Peter used
the remote to switch off the TV. Van clicked off the
bedside lamp. Indigo darkness poured through the
window, filling the room with the hue of the night sky.

"Good night," Van murmured to Peter.

"Good night," Peter murmured back.

Van took out his hearing aids and set them on his
bedside table. Velvety quiet took their place.

In the darkness and the silence, Van's thoughts
drifted outward, tracing a line of knots that tied him to
one person, and another, and another. In spite of the
burping, and the jokes, and the amber, he still wasn't
sure that he could trust Peter. But he had no choice.
Pebble probably didn't trust Van completely either, but
she had to rely on him for help. Van wasn't sure that
they could trust the Collectors to do the right thing

when it came to Wish Eaters, and the Collectors almost certainly felt the same way about him. Maybe this was what happened when problems grew too big for someone to solve them alone. Maybe you had to take the risk of relying on someone else.

Van glanced over at Peter, watching the blankets rise and fall with Peter's deep, peaceful breaths. Then he burrowed under his covers and let his own eyes slide shut.

12
Pebble's Past

The Greys left late Sunday morning.

Peter gave Van a last wave through the window of the sleek black car. Van waved back, hope and worry fluttering in his chest like two fighting birds.

For the rest of that day, and the next, and the next, Van stayed inside the converted stables while Fox Den Opera surged into high gear. Preparation for the season-opening production of *Hansel and Gretel* had taken over every inch of the grounds. Even in his bedroom, with the windows closed and the door shut, Van could catch the roar of trucks on the drive, the buzz of construction on the stage, the shouting of staff members hurrying by.

But the nights were as silent as ever.

On Wednesday night, Van lay half asleep in bed, trying to feel comfortable in the stillness, when a band of light slashed across his ceiling.

Van jerked backward. His head thumped the wall.

The light slashed again. It swept back and forth across the room, illuminating patches of wall and floor and bed before landing blindingly in Van's eyes.

Van squinted into it.

It was the beam of a flashlight. It was coming through his window. And aiming it, outlined by pale moonlight, was a familiar figure.

Van stumbled out of bed, pushed his hearing aids into his ears, and flung the window open.

". . . Come out and talk?" said Pebble.

Van nodded. Tugging a cardigan over his pajamas, he clambered out the low window.

Pebble led the way to the edge of the woods, where they could huddle without being seen. She aimed the flashlight at the ground.

". . . Get to it?" she asked, speaking too fast for Van to comb the words out of the sound. ". . . Take them inside?"

"The message?" Van repeated. "I took care of it."

Even in the dimness, he could see Pebble's shoulders relax. "Good," she breathed. "So they're coming?"

"I don't know. I think so."

Pebble's head cocked. ". . . Din tell you?"

"Well . . . ," said Van. "I couldn't get to the city myself. I *tried*. So I had to send the message with somebody else instead."

"What?" Pebble's voice was like the edge of a saw. "With *who*?"

"With a friend," said Van, wondering if "friend" was the right word for Peter. "I mean—with the boy I had been staying with. He doesn't know what the message said. He doesn't know about the Collection. He was just going to deliver it to the collection agency office and leave."

Pebble let out a breath so fiery it almost made Van's eyes water. "You can't—" She broke off, her voice shaking. "You can't just *trust* people like that!"

"But sometimes you *have* to trust people," said Van. "You trusted *me*."

". . . Maybe it's not good enough," Pebble muttered. Or it might have been *Maybe I shouldn't have*.

Either way, the words stung.

"Can I hold the flashlight?" Van asked. "So I can see your face?"

Pebble passed it over, mumbling *sure* or *sorry* or something else.

Van pointed the light at her. In the beam, she looked rumpled and tired, with faint pink edges around her eyes.

"I know you can't trust everybody," said Van. "But there are lots of people who are good. Or they're good enough."

Pebble was silent for a moment. It was the kind of silence that meant something else was coming—like the inhalation before a scream.

". . . Know why I left Uncle Ivor for the Collectors?" she said at last.

"No," Van answered. "Why?"

"Because people who say they want to help you always want something else too."

"What do you mean?"

Pebble's mossy-penny eyes fixed on the ground. She spoke slowly, as though she were digging up words from someplace where they'd been buried for a long time. "Uncle Ivor kept me shut in the house for the first eight years of my life."

"What?" said Van, even though he was quite sure he hadn't misunderstood. "Like . . . you could never go outside? Not even to school?"

"Not even in the *yard*," said Pebble. "He kept all the

doors locked and the curtains shut. I never saw a single person except for Uncle Ivor, Hans and Gerda, and the people on TV. Sometimes I'd go to sleep, and I'd wake up in the same bed, but in a different room in some other city or country. And that house would be all locked up too."

"But . . . why?"

Pebble's voice grew sharp. "Because the Collectors couldn't know about me. They knew all about *him*, but they had no idea that he'd wished me. That I even existed." She let the words hang for a moment. "He said it was to keep me safe. But that wasn't all it was."

Van wanted to reach out for her, but Pebble looked a bit too prickly to touch. "Was it really lonely?" he asked instead.

She shrugged one shoulder. "I had Uncle Ivor and Hans and Gerda. That's what I was used to. That's all I thought I needed."

Pebble's words slid into Van like a key into a lock.

For most of his life—until he'd met Pebble and Barnavelt and Lemmy—Van had had his mother, and no one else. The two of them traveled the world, alone but together. Like Pebble, Van had fallen asleep in one room or city or country and woken up in another more times than he could count. But then, in each new place, he and his mother would put on their shoes and head out to explore. They would visit castles and museums and parks. They'd try out a dozen shops, looking for the very best gelato.

Thinking of Pebble, trapped in a moving cage, made Van feel luckier than he'd ever felt.

"Uncle Ivor tried to make it nice," Pebble went on. "He let me help with the Wish Eaters. And of course we could wish for anything we wanted. I had rooms full of toys. I had pet lizards. I had a pinball arcade. And Uncle Ivor had his collections."

Pebble shifted, leaning against a fallen tree. Van perched on a stump beside her. He focused the light and his eyes on her face, following every word.

"But then one day, when I was eight years old, Uncle Ivor took me out into the backyard." Pebble's face shifted, a strange smile curling the corners of her mouth. "I still remember how the ground felt under my shoes. So different from wood or carpet. And I remember the air, how it was always moving, even when there wasn't any wind. How the sun fell through the leaves." She glanced up at the leaves, where nothing fell through now but inky darkness.

"We were at the house in the city. Uncle Ivor sat me down by the fountain. There were Wish Eaters in the trees around us. *They* got to be outside, and I didn't." Pebble's smile turned bitter. "Uncle Ivor told me I was finally old enough to do some really important work. I could help him and the Wish Eaters. All I had to do was keep my eyes open, and not tell anyone about him. I said okay." Pebble shifted uncomfortably, patting at her sides with both hands like she was searching for coat pockets to slide them into. "Hans put me in the car and drove me through the city. I'd never been in a car before. I just stared out the window the whole time, because I couldn't believe how big the city was. How many *people* there were. Hans stopped at a corner and told me to get out of the car. So I did. And then he drove away."

"What?" said Van. "He just left you there?"

Pebble nodded. "I didn't know what to do. I didn't know where I was. I didn't even know our address. All these people were driving past me, walking around me, bumping into me, and it was like—like they couldn't even see me."

"What happened?" Van asked.

"I just stood there for a long time, because I didn't

know where to go. I was crying. Nobody stopped to help me. But then I noticed this—this squirrel." Pebble's lips twitched. "This pale gray squirrel. It sat on a wire above me, keeping perfectly still, just staring and staring at me. So I stared back. Because at least *somebody* could see me." She paused, gazing at an empty branch above. "Then the squirrel jumped down and squeezed through an open window into this little office building . . . so I ran after it."

"Into the Collection," Van breathed.

"Sesame caught me in the entry chamber," said Pebble. "But when she saw how scared I was, she was nice to me. She gave me a handkerchief, because my face was all wet, and a big warm coat to wear, because I was cold. She told me her name. And I met Nail and Jack and a bunch of others, and the squirrel climbed up onto my shoulder and said his name was Barnavelt."

"Were you surprised?" Van asked. "To hear a squirrel talk?"

"I'd never seen a real squirrel before." Pebble gave a sheepish smile. "I thought maybe they all talked. Anyway, the grown-ups were trying to decide what to do. They didn't know who I was or why I could see them, and I was trying to listen and look around at the same time, and the place was so big and there were so many people . . . and then there was this huge crashing sound from the street up above. It was so loud, it made the walls shake. Stones started falling from the ceiling."

"What was it?" Van asked.

"The grown-ups all ran up the stairs to see, and I went with them. There had been an explosion across the street. A whole building had collapsed. The street was full of dust and smoke and screaming, and there was silver wish mist everywhere." Pebble swallowed. "Everybody was rushing around, shouting at each other. Nobody noticed when Hans and Gerda pulled up to the curb and yanked me into the car."

"So . . . Mr. Falborg used a wish?"

Pebble nodded. "He needed a distraction to get me safely home again. But other people got hurt." She tugged at her sweater. "Before that, I hadn't realized that sometimes wishes made bad things happen. That when you make a wish, you risk hurting someone else with the way it comes true."

Van thought of the garbage truck roaring across the sidewalk inches from his body. He thought of his mother, lying broken on the street. He held the flashlight steady and waited for Pebble to go on.

"When I got home, Uncle Ivor was so excited that his plan to get me into the Collection had worked. He asked me a million questions. He said that now that I had gotten inside the Collection, I could go back again and learn even more. He wanted me to find out about the trapped Wish Eaters, where they were, how they were kept. He wanted me to find out about the collected wishes. And he wanted—he wanted me to steal a dead wish."

"A dead wish?" Van repeated. "Why?"

"Because they're the most powerful. They're pure magic. And because Uncle Ivor can make all the wishes that he wants, but he can't collect other peoples' wishes. He can't create a *dead* wish. Like I said, he isn't a Collector."

Pebble paused for a moment, staring into Van's face, before continuing.

"The next day, Hans drove me back to the Collection, and I sneaked inside. But this time . . . I don't know." Her voice faltered. "These people had been nice to me. They *saw* me. I didn't want to spy on them or steal from them. I didn't know what to do. In the end, it didn't even matter, because somewhere way down that staircase, in the dark . . . I got lost."

Van knew that darkness well. The chilly dampness of the air. The terrible, wall-rumbling roars that came from the Hold below. In the beam of his flashlight, he saw Pebble shiver, and knew she was remembering those things too. "What happened?" he breathed.

"Nail found me."

"Was he angry?"

Pebble shook her head. "He was . . . he was *nice*." A smile moved the corners of her mouth. "The Collectors had figured out almost everything about me by then. They knew I'd been sent there. They knew who sent me. But Nail didn't ask about any of that. He just explained what the Collectors did, and why. He let me see the Holders containing a giant Wish Eater. He showed me the Collection. He explained about dead wishes, and why they're so dangerous. The more he talked, the more I realized how many people Uncle Ivor and I might have hurt just by wishing. How many things we might have messed up without even knowing it.

"Of course when I got home, Uncle Ivor wanted to know everything I'd learned," Pebble went on. "But I wouldn't tell him anything. Except that I wasn't ever going to spy for him again."

A breeze whisked through the woods, sending its cold

fingers down the collar of Van's shirt. "Was *he* angry?"

"Uncle Ivor doesn't get angry. He just gets *disappointed*." There was bitterness in Pebble's voice now. "He couldn't believe that I would betray him. That I'd forgotten where I belonged. Who I belonged to." She stiffened, as though the words still chafed her. "He said I had put us in danger, and we would be leaving the next day, and I would never see the city again. He said he'd been wrong to let me out in the first place. And then he locked me in my bedroom."

Van stared at Pebble, waiting. He realized that he'd clenched both hands, as though he himself was about to pound desperately at a locked door.

"It was late at night when I heard a little voice at the window." Another small, fragile smile started to pull at Pebble's mouth. "Barnavelt had come for me."

"What did you do?"

Pebble's smile opened wider. "I used my bedside lamp to break the glass in the window."

"Didn't anybody notice?"

"Probably. But I was out of the house by then." Her smile was bright and steady now. "Barnavelt and I climbed down a tree. I'd never even touched a tree before. I'd never been outside at night. I'd never gotten to just run and run and run. Barnavelt led the way through the city. I remember there were animals everywhere—squirrels, rats, pigeons, cats. There was moonlight on the river. There were so many stars. It was all so big, and now I was part of it. And when we got to the Collection, it was—it was like they had all been waiting for me." Tears sparkled in Pebble's eyes. "Hundreds of people—and they all knew who I was. They gave me a new name. I was one of them."

"So that's how you left," said Van, after a silent moment. "No wonder Mr. Falborg wanted you to come back."

"I didn't do it to hurt him," said Pebble, almost as if she were explaining this to Mr. Falborg himself. "I think he really believed—at least partly—that by locking me in, he was keeping me safe."

"Just like he does with the Wish Eaters."

"Yeah," said Pebble. "He loves them too." She raised her head, meeting Van's eyes. "But what he's doing is wrong. It's all a big mistake. I want to stop him before he does something *really* dangerous."

"The Collectors will come," said Van, with more certainty than he felt. "They'll get the message. They'll be here."

Another breeze whipped through the woods. Van shivered.

Pebble's face hardened suddenly. Her louder, sharper voice returned. "I'd better get back. You should too." She pushed herself away from the fallen tree. Van put the flashlight in her waiting hand, losing her face in the flickering shadows.

"Van." Pebble's voice spoke through the darkness. ". . . Sorry . . . mixed up in this."

"I'm not sorry," said Van, without even having to think. "I mean, I'm sorry my mother got hurt. But everything else . . . I wouldn't take anything back."

Pebble's silhouette held very still for a moment. Something brushed Van's arm—something like the touch of a hand. But Pebble was already turning away.

"See you Friday!" she called over her shoulder.

Then she rushed away, the trees folding around her.

Back in his own room, Van couldn't sleep.

He knelt beside his miniature stage, lining up a row of dinosaurs and dragons and sparkling bits of jewelry behind the White Wizard. They faced off against a mass of robots and toy animals and miniature soldiers. SuperVan and Pawn Girl stood between the enemy lines.

No one moved.

No one spoke.

For as long as Van knelt there, his head growing heavier and his eyes growing sleepier, the two sides faced off in perfect stillness.

Finally Van crawled into bed. He turned his head so he couldn't see the stage anymore, or think about the battle that might come, or wonder which side would finally win.

13
Meet Mabel

"Très charmant," said Van's mother, straightening the ends of his bow tie.

Unless *"charmant"* meant uncomfortable, Van wasn't sure he agreed. "Do I have to get all dressed up even if I'm not going to the opera?"

"You're attending the gala reception with me," said his mother, giving Van's white shirt and gray vest a final tweak. "There will be scores of people who want to see you. And Giovanni, are you *sure* you don't want to stay for the performance? You already know the story of Hansel and Gretel, and the music is lovely."

Van glanced down at the festival program lying on the kitchen table. "The composer's actual name is Engelbert Humperdinck?"

"Yes, that was his actual name." His mother swished toward the entryway mirror and adjusted a pin in her upswept hair. She smoothed the folds of her green silk gown—the one that made her look like a giant melted emerald. "People can't help what they're named, Giovanni."

"They can't help their *last* names. His parents didn't have to name him Engelbert."

His mother sighed. "All right, *caro mio. Andiamo.*" She held out her arm for Van to take, and the two of them stepped out the door.

The gala season opening had begun. The Fox Den driveways swarmed with running valets and arriving cars. A string quartet played in the gardens. The grounds blossomed with operagoers in bright clothes. And beyond them, on every side, the woods waved softly.

It was Friday evening at last.

His mother steered him toward the festival tent. People sauntered in and out, laughing, calling to one another, sipping from sparkling glasses. The moment Van and his mother entered, every head turned.

"Ingrid!" someone shouted. "Ingrid, darling!"

In another instant, Ingrid Markson was surrounded by fans and friends, and Van was several feet deep in a pool of babbling grown-ups. He craned around someone's elbow. Far away, he could see the edge of the woods—the woods where the wishing well and its hidden Eater waited, surrounded by moss and shadows.

But if everything went according to plan, the Eater wouldn't stay hidden for long.

A thread of anticipation shot through him. Just a couple of hours . . .

"Lovely to see you!" his mother was singing to a bunch of people Van didn't recognize, grasping hands and kissing cheeks. "So glad you're here! . . . *Darling!* It's been too long!"

Van stopped trying to follow the conversation. He kept his eyes on the forest, drifting on the flood of noise and names that whirled around him. But then his mother shouted a name that he recognized. A name that plunged him straight down into the freezing dark.

"Why, *Mr. Falborg!*"

Van's heart stuttered.

Could he have heard wrong? Was his mind playing tricks on him? As though his body was stuck in slow motion, Van turned toward the target of his mother's voice.

And there he was.

Ivor Falborg.

Opera aficionado. Curio collector. Van's almost-murderer.

Mr. Falborg looked crisp and elegant in his customary white suit. His eyes were blue and crinkly. His smile was warm.

It filled Van's bones with ice.

"Signorina Markson!" Mr. Falborg bowed over her hand. "How glorious to see you. If only you were gracing us with your voice, this evening would be perfect."

Van's mother laughed her bell-like laugh. "You're *too* kind!" She gave Van's shoulder a squeeze. "Giovanni, it's Mr. Falborg, our friend from the city! What a lovely surprise!"

Van swallowed something that felt like a fistful of shattered glass. "Huh . . . hello," he rasped.

"Do you come to the Fox Den regularly?" sang his mother.

"Every fall season," said Mr. Falborg, his own smile gliding back and forth between Van and his mother as easily as if he chatted with his attempted murder victims and their parents every day. ". . . a little country place . . . not far from here. I'm currently living there with my niece. Please, let me introduce you to my Mabel."

He gestured to the person hiding behind him.

And there was Pebble.

Sort of.

Her usual sloppy ponytail had been swept into a shiny knob on the back of her head and encircled by little blossoms on bobby pins. A fussy white dress with a yellow sash puffed around her. Instead of sneakers, her feet were strapped into stiff white sandals. If she hadn't had Pebble's mossy-penny eyes, with Pebble's personality glaring straight out of them, she would barely have been Pebble at all.

Van had seen cats in Halloween costumes who looked more comfortable than Pebble did at that moment.

He made a sound that wanted to be a laugh but came out as a muffled *snurk* instead.

"Lovely to meet you, Mabel," said Van's mother, leaning over to take Pebble's hand. She gave Van a bump with her elbow. "Giovanni, say hello."

Van had to chew on his lips for a second. "Nice to meet you, *Mabel*," he managed.

Pebble's eyes narrowed. "Nice to meet you, *Giovanni*."

Mr. Falborg stood beside them, still beaming as though this were just a lovely late summer day at an opera festival. Of course, Mr. Falborg knew that Van and Pebble already knew each other. He knew they had worked together on the side of the Collectors. He knew "Mabel" had another, realer name. But he obviously felt so secure in Pebble's loyalty—or at least in his power over her—that he could bring her here, straight to her old friend and ally, without even a waver in his crinkly smile.

Something about this made Van's stomach hurt.

"Well. We ought to let you greet your other admirers," said Mr. Falborg to Van's mother. He beamed at both of them again. "Good day, Signorina and Signor Markson." With a last bow, he ushered Pebble away.

Van's mother turned toward a knot of waiting fans. Van was left alone, gulping deep breaths, waiting for the ice in his spine to thaw. Could Pebble have been right about her uncle? Might his own near-murder have been nothing but an accident, a wish gone wrong? And how much did that matter? If someone kept a child locked up for eight years because he imagined that could keep the child safe, did that make it all right?

It was hard to think. The tent was growing even louder, voices pummeling Van's head like mallets on a timpani. He had crept as far into one corner as he could go without tripping over any tent posts when somebody grabbed his elbow.

"Hey," Pebble whispered. Her words were swamped by noise. ". . . staying in . . . opera?"

"What? No, I'm not staying," Van answered. "Are you?"

Pebble shook her head. "In ten . . . all pretend . . . stomachache." A funny expression tugged at her face. "You see the composer's name?"

Van grinned back at her. "Engelbert Humperdinck. It sounds like the punch line of a joke you'd get in trouble for telling."

Pebble snickered, covering her mouth with one hand. "Right," she said, stiffening again. ". . . edge of the woods when the show starts. See you then."

She darted back into the crowd.

Moments later, when a hand grabbed his arm again, Van wondered what else Pebble had to tell him. Maybe she'd thought of the perfect joke for the punch line of Engelbert Humperdinck.

He spun around, eager to hear it.

But the hand on his arm wasn't Pebble's. It was his mother's.

And the eyes staring back at him weren't Pebble's either.

They were the ice-water eyes of Peter Grey.

14
Peter and the Woods

"Giovanni, look who it is!" His mother's voice chimed over the crowd. "Charles and Peter are here!"

Mr. Grey, looking even snootier than usual in a pearl-gray suit, murmured something that Van couldn't catch. He and Van's mother clasped hands and kissed each other on the cheeks. Peter turned away from the kissing, looking mildly ill.

Van swayed on his feet.

Peter Grey. Peter Grey and his father. Here. Tonight. Along with Pebble and Mr. Falborg and—hopefully—a bunch of incoming Collectors and an ancient wish-eating monster. Van felt as though he'd just swallowed a week's worth of meals at once.

"What a joy to see you again so soon!" Van's

mother went on. "I had no idea you would be here!"

Mr. Grey smiled back at her. "Thought we saw an opening for separating you two."

No, thought Van. He couldn't have said that. He must have said something about *opening performance* and *surprising you two*. Still, the look Mr. Grey was giving his mother made Van want to dive between them and do some separating of his own.

"I'm so glad I'll have company for the performance!" his mother exclaimed. "I can't convince Giovanni to attend with me. He would rather sit in our rooms and read comic books." Her eyebrows rose. "Perhaps Peter would enjoy that too! Peter, would you rather spend the evening with Giovanni than be stuck with a bunch of stuffy old adults?"

Peter's face brightened.

"No!" Van shouted.

His mother and Mr. Grey turned to look down at him. Mr. Grey looked annoyed. His mother looked stunned.

The expression that had lightened Peter's face disappeared in an instant, leaving it as cool and hard as a marble floor.

"That's all right," said Peter, before anyone else

could speak. His eyes stayed away from Van. "I want to see the opera."

"Oh, you'll love this production." Van's mother rushed to cover the awkwardness. "The choreography is simply *sublime* . . ."

"Mom?" Van interrupted desperately. "Can Peter and I go get a lemonade?"

"Of course!" his mother sang. "Enjoy yourselves!"

Van grabbed Peter by the sleeve. He dragged him to a far corner of the tent, feeling—strangely—more like Pebble than he'd ever felt.

"I'm really sorry," Van said, once they stood face-to-face in the quieter spot. "It's not that I don't want to be with you. It's just . . . I have something else I need to do tonight."

"Another dangerous secret you can't tell me about?" Peter's voice was chilly. "Fine. I took your message to that weird office, by the way. As soon as I got back to the city. And I didn't open it, if you were wondering."

"Thank you," breathed Van. "And I wasn't wondering."

Beyond the walls of the tent, the sky was beginning to dim. Lengthening rays of sun seared the gardens with gold, and the fountains glittered, scattering droplets that winked like burning sparks. Along the paths that wound toward the open-air stage, strings of fairy lights began to twinkle on.

"I'd explain everything if I could," Van rushed on. "It's just—they're not *my* secrets. They're somebody else's. I—"

But as Van spoke, a change swept through the tent. Operagoers set down their glasses and surged toward the lighted paths. Peter turned away.

"Wait. What is it?" Van asked, grabbing Peter by the sleeve again.

"They played the fanfare," said Peter. "Didn't you hear it?"

Without waiting for an answer, Peter turned and strode off.

Van scanned the receding crowd. His mother was leaving the tent on Mr. Grey's arm, the two of them beaming at each other like this entire party was for them. The instant they were out of sight, Van spun around, ducked underneath the tent wall, and bolted for the woods.

Ahead of him, the puff of Pebble's dress glowed against the shadows. As Van raced closer, he could see that she had already demolished her shiny bun and pulled her hair into its usual sloppy ponytail. Bobby pins and tiny white blossoms lay scattered in the grass around her.

"He did it," Van panted, jogging to a stop. "Peter delivered the message. The Collectors should be coming."

". . . guess we'll see," said Pebble shortly. "Come on."

They plunged into the trees.

The path from the Fox Den to the well was far longer than the one from the Falborg mansion. The sky darkened above them as they ran, turning from deep blue to murky violet. The first tiny stars appeared, glimmering in gaps in the canopy, their light too weak to press through.

Van kept his eyes sharp, scanning the trees on every side, watching Pebble's ponytail bob ahead of him. The hem of her dress was already splotched with mud. Her sandals had gone from white to brown. Van pictured her, locked for years inside Mr. Falborg's fancy homes, buttoned into fancy clothes, forced to live as a girl named Mabel, when the real Pebble must have been there all along.

A gust of cold, damp air slid down his back. Van glanced around. There was nothing behind him. But a few feet away, a branch swung back and forth too forcefully to have been pushed by the wind.

Van scrambled closer to Pebble.

They passed the Falborg mansion, keeping deep within the trees. The peak of its tower loomed above them, thrusting like a knife into the sky. Without speaking, they ran faster.

But the night fell faster still.

By the time they reached the clearing, the sky was blue black. They stumbled onto the grass, gasping.

The well waited for them. Dampness shimmered on its stones. Moss blanketed its roof, and tiny white mushrooms glowed all around it like the crumbs of fallen stars. When Van stood still, he could feel it: the faint, trembling motion of something far below. Something alive.

Pebble dove through a patch of ferns and pulled out an armload of flashlights. She passed Van two of them.

"Now what?" Van asked as Pebble switched on two flashlights of her own.

His heart was thumping too hard and Pebble was too out of breath for him to catch her answer, but it sounded like *up*. Or, maybe, *hope*.

Pebble aimed her flashlight beams at the sky. Van did the same. The sky was so vast and so deep, their little lights seemed useless—like four tiny arms trying to stir the ocean. But Pebble didn't stop. So Van didn't either. He glanced over at her, watching her profile against the thickening shadows for a moment, before looking up again.

A small, dark blot had appeared in the sky.

Van stared at it. At first it was so small and so dark that he couldn't see *it* at all, but only the sky that disappeared behind it. Then it began to grow, dropping lower, until he could make out a dense, casketlike shape—like a black train car without wheels. Above the casket, lashed to it by strands that glinted in the starlight, were two more shapes. These were huge and silvery, half hidden in swathes of net. But Van could tell two things.

They were alive. And they were coming fast.

Pebble touched his arm. ". . . the carriage," she breathed.

The flying shape loomed closer. It blotted out a patch of stars that grew and grew, like a widening hole, until at last the dark thing itself came plummeting down into the clearing.

Van and Pebble staggered back. Van stumbled on a lump in the ground, dropping his flashlights as he caught himself. They rolled off into the grass.

The dark shape landed just inches away. It hit the

ground so heavily that its edges sank into the earth. Up close, in the shaking beam of Pebble's flashlights, Van saw that it *did* look a lot like an unwheeled train car—one made of black metal, with narrow, glassless windows lining its sides. A hatch jutted from its top, where three drivers controlled a mass of iron spikes and glinting ropes. And above the carriage, bound by spiderweb nets and prodded by those spikes, were two monstrous Wish Eaters.

The drivers dragged the Eaters downward until they hovered just above the grass before the carriage. Then they drove iron stakes through the loops of rope, pinning the beasts to the ground. The Eaters howled.

A door in the carriage burst open.

A man stepped out.

His hulking shape filled the doorway. His black leather coat swept the grass. Straps of glinting metal hooks crossed his back, and silvery ropes coiled over his shoulder. His sharp black eyes—one of them twisted slightly by the deep scar that curved from his eyelid all the way to his jaw—fell on Van.

His face split into a warm smile.

"Well," said Razor, the master of the Hold. "It's a good trip that ends with finding you two."

15
The Plot

Razor stepped aside. Other Collectors poured out of the carriage: several of Razor's Holders, Jack and his fellow guards, and one tall, gray-haired man with rats on his shoulders.

Nail stepped into the clearing. His rats, sniffing the air, suddenly went still. Nail's gaze fell on Pebble.

Before he could speak, Pebble plunged into an explanation. "Uncle Ivor . . . rest of the evening . . . have it contained . . ." She spoke faster and faster, dropping her flashlights and clutching anxiously as her skirt instead. ". . . in time. But I didn't know if you'd think . . . ," she added, slowing down at last. "I wasn't sure you'd come."

Nail stepped closer to her. If he spoke, Van couldn't

catch the words. Nail opened his arms and wrapped Pebble up inside them. The rest of the Collectors surged closer. Pebble disappeared in a mass of embraces and long dark coats.

At the same moment, a small, silvery shape scuttled out of the carriage and bounded onto its roof, overlooking them all.

Van watched the squirrel search the crowd. Its eyes locked on something. Its body went still.

"Pebble!" Barnavelt squealed.

Pebble's head whipped up. "Barnavelt!" she shouted back.

The squirrel dove into the crowd, bouncing off Collectors' heads. "Pebble, is it really you? Are you *sure* it's you?" Barnavelt made the final leap to Pebble's shoulder. He pressed against the side of her neck, sniffing loudly. "Oh. It *is* you," he said, clearly relieved. "But Pebble, *what* are you *wearing*?"

Van heard the ripple of laughter. The circle of dark coats closed around Pebble again.

An unexpected emptiness opened inside Van's heart.

Of course Pebble was still a Collector. Of course they welcomed her back. He was glad for her, and at the same time, her being fully one of them once more left Van alone, on the edge, not quite sure where he belonged. If he belonged anywhere at all.

At last, the knot of Collectors broke apart. Several people spoke at once. Van caught the words *well, Eater, trap.* Razor gave commands to the other Holders, who unloaded vicious hooks and spikes and yards and yards of spiderweb net from within the carriage. Nail murmured with Pebble, occasionally turning his head to listen to the rats whispering in his ears.

Behind Van, something moaned. He jerked around.

At the edge of the clearing, the harnessed, hooded Wish Eaters tugged weakly at their ropes. The Eaters were huge—terrifyingly huge—but that moan had been sad and small, like the sound a captured animal makes as it sits alone in its cage.

Van's stomach began to hurt. He turned back toward the preparing Collectors.

With their nets and weapons ready, the Holders formed a ring around the well. Starlight glimmered on the tips of their iron hooks. Their spiderweb nets seemed almost to glow.

Pebble and Barnavelt backed out of the way. Nail stepped to the side of the well.

For the next moment, no one moved. Stillness settled

over the clearing. The Collectors stood like sculptures in dark stone, motionless except for the occasional ripple of a wind-stirred coat.

Van froze too. He held his breath. He concentrated on the earth beneath his feet, trying to feel the tremble from deep underground that he had felt before. But even the ground kept still. He wondered if the Collectors had forgotten all about him. He wondered what he was doing here, and whether he should run away without ever seeing the awful thing hidden in the well, or what the Holders and their hooks would do to it. He wondered why he couldn't decide.

After a moment so long that Van started to think it would never end, Nail broke the stillness. He reached down and drew something from one of his coat's many pockets, setting it on the rim of the well.

It was a green glass bottle. The starry light sealed inside of it pulsed softly.

A wish, Van thought.

"To lure the Eater out," answered a tiny voice that spoke directly to Van's mind.

Small, tickling paws scrambled up Van's body. Nail's rats settled themselves on his shoulders.

"Violetta. Raduslav," Van whispered, feeling surprisingly

grateful to have two big black rats pressed against his neck. "Did you come to keep me company?"

"Yes," said Violetta, the higher-voiced rat.

"And no," said Raduslav, in his slightly lower voice. "Also safer back here."

"But a decent view," added Violetta.

The three of them stared across the clearing at the pulsing green light.

"What is Nail doing with the wish?" Van asked.

"Must offer what it wants to eat," said Violetta.

"But the Eater won't eat," Raduslav put in. "Will be caught first."

"Will they really be able to catch something this big?" whispered Van.

"They will," said Raduslav. "Or they won't."

"One or the other," agreed Violetta.

Reaching into his pockets again, Nail placed another glowing wish on the rim of the well, this one in a larger, paler bottle. The Holders shifted, clutching their weapons.

But if the bait was working, there was no sign. The hole of the well remained black and empty. The ground beneath their feet kept still. As the Collectors stared into the well, something high and far off caught the corner of Van's eye. He glanced up. In the sky above the Fox Den, a golden glow hung in the air. *Those must be the lights of the outdoor stage,* Van reasoned, as another burst of gold reached toward the stars.

A flicker of motion yanked his attention back to the well. Nail muttered something to the nearest Collectors. The circle around the well edged backward, a new, heavy tension hanging in the air.

One of the Holders took a metal box from the carriage. The others stood back as he approached the well, holding the box carefully in both hands. Nail unlatched its lid. Eerie reddish light poured from within.

Nail removed a third bottled wish—a wish with a color Van had never seen before. It looked like a lit coal, but brighter, or like a jewel of burning blood.

"What is that?" Van breathed.

"Dead wish," Raduslav whispered back. "Eater won't be able to resist."

The harnessed Eaters moaned again. This time, Van felt an answering shiver in the ground beneath him. Invisible frost flashed through him, freezing his lungs. The thing at the bottom of the well was stirring.

"It feels," said Violetta softly.

"What—what does it feel?" Van managed.

JACQUELINE WEST

"Feels *us*," the rat answered.

A rush of wind raked through the clearing. The Collectors' black coats billowed. Gathered tight around the well, they looked like a flock of blackbirds perched on the carcass of something newly dead.

"Will they hurt it?" Van whispered to the rats. "If they can't just catch it, will they—"

He was interrupted by a roar.

Van jumped. The rats scrabbled at his shoulders.

But the roar hadn't come from the depths of the well. It had come from the edge of the clearing.

Van spun to look.

The harnessed Wish Eaters were in a frenzy. Their bodies thrashed against the ropes. A handful of Holders broke from the well and rushed to control them, gouging them with iron hooks. The Eaters howled.

Sickened, Van turned from the Eaters to the well, to the bottled wishes twinkling there, just out of the starving beings' reach. If the wishes were enough to lure an ancient Eater, of course they would tempt these beasts too. For a blink, Van imagined dashing forward to grab the bottles and giving the poor things what they wanted. But when he turned back toward the Eaters, he saw that they weren't facing the well at all.

★182★

They were craning toward a spot in the distance.

Toward the same spot where Van had seen the glow in the sky.

The glow above the Fox Den had grown brighter. Now, as Van watched, pink and violet bursts tinged the air above the trees. Swirls of silvery mist rose around them. A falling star streaked across the blackness, its trail as solid and bright as the blade of a knife.

"Oh no," whispered Violetta.

"Oh no, no no," added Raduslav.

The Eaters screamed.

One of them bucked its cloak of nets aside, revealing the head of a skeletal horse. Leathery wings sprouted from its back. The monster bellowed, sharp silver teeth gleaming.

Van staggered backward. He barely felt the rats jumping from his shoulders, barely noticed them bolting through the grass toward Nail. The creature's roar clanged inside Van's skull.

The other Eater kicked at the restraints, managing to rise a few feet from the ground. Two Holders were dragged off their feet. More Collectors ran to help. Van scuttled away from the fray. Across the clearing, through a mass of moving bodies, he glimpsed Pebble standing a few steps from the well, and saw Nail setting the dead wish back in its locked metal box.

A burst of blue light, this one so bright that it singed the air of the clearing, flashed from the direction of the Fox Den. The carriage made an earth-tearing lurch. Nail shouted for Razor. Razor shouted back, his reply lost in an Eater's roar.

The Holders behind Van were shouting something too. Van thought he caught the words *media show.*

He repeated them to himself.

Media show. Media show.

Meteor shower.

Chaos surged through the clearing.

The Holders abandoned the thrashing Eaters, who had nearly freed themselves from the spiderweb ropes. Gathering up their weapons and nets, the Holders raced into the trees, toward the strange light.

Another meteor sliced across the sky. Mist, so thick that Van could almost taste it, billowed across the treetops.

Pebble's familiar grip closed around Van's arm. Behind them, Razor's deep voice gave a last command.

"That way!" he shouted, pointing toward the Fox Den. *"RUN!"*

16
Intermission

The curtain closed on act 2 of Engelbert Humperdinck's *Hansel and Gretel*. The audience rose to its feet for intermission, following the fairy-lighted aisles to the grounds, where they could wander until act 3 began.

It was a perfect late summer night. The fountains around Fox Den sparkled. Breezes brushed the gardens, carrying away the scent of roses. Except for the wisps of silvery mist that stopped some distance from the stage, settling on the grass like cottonwood seeds, the air was as clear as glass.

Someone spotted a shooting star.

Clusters of people glanced up. There were oohs and ahhs. Some of the operagoers applauded, as though this were another part of the show. For a moment, faintly enough that no one noticed, the air thickened with fast-falling dew.

And then the phones began to ring.

"What? I got the job?"

"She was accepted? I *knew* it!"

"You're getting married? Oh, darling, that's wonderful!"

The wisps of silvery mist drifted closer, although now there was no breeze.

Another falling star streaked above.

Thousands of rose petals rained down over the gardens. A bald man scurried away from the crowd, blinded by the fast-growing hair already hanging in front of his eyes. Backstage, the soprano playing Gretel came down with a coughing fit so violent that she could barely breathe. She was still coughing when her secretively smiling understudy was hustled into Gretel's costume.

The wisps of mist grew larger. Still, no one in the crowd seemed to see.

Three more falling stars sliced the sky. The air billowed with fog.

Five limousines roared up the drive. One popped its trunk, spilling a pile of chocolate bonbons. Another opened its doors to release a pack of purebred Pomeranians.

Fireworks burst above the outdoor stage. Sparks rained down above the operagoers, who smiled and cooed in happy surprise. Some of the cinders landed harmlessly in the damp grass. A few touched down near the seats, where ushers raced to stomp them out. And several hit the canvas tent.

In a breath, it was on fire.

Staff rushed for water. Operagoers gasped and ran. A woman in a dress like a melted emerald staggered as she hurried away from the fire, a painful limp nearly making her fall. The gray-suited man beside her caught her arm.

Another star shot across the sky.

A streak of mist snaked close to the woman, swallowing the spark of light that rose, unseen, just above her.

The woman halted.

"Charles," she gasped. "My leg. I—I can't believe it." She took another two steps. "It feels like it was never broken at all!"

Laughing with joy, the woman threw her arms around the man. They held each other close for a moment. Then the man held up one hand, and the two of them whirled into a waltz.

Four more stars fell.

A silvery hot air balloon touched down in the gardens, tangled a nearby couple in its ropes, and whisked them, screaming, into the sky. A fistfight broke out. Someone discovered a knife in his belt that hadn't been there a moment before. Someone else found a sword.

In the drive, horns honked and engines roared. There were crashes. Breaking glass and clashing metal. Angry yells.

Amid the confusion, a boy with ice-water eyes climbed a small rise in the ground. He'd been left alone at the outdoor stage. Now he searched the crowd until he found the man in the gray suit, dancing with the woman in the melted emerald dress. He watched them for a long moment, wishing that, just for one night, somebody might notice *him*.

A final falling star shot across the sky.

A blast of wind tore over the grounds. Behind the boy, a post holding a heavy rack of lights began to splinter. With a crack that was lost in the noise of the crowd, the top half of the post plunged down.

It struck the boy from above. He fell, unmoving, into the dark grass.

The man in the gray suit turned with a start. "Peter?" he shouted. He raced up the slope. *"Peter?"*

The burning tent crackled. People fought and danced and cheered and screamed. Somewhere, an alarm began to wail.

Meanwhile, beyond the reach of the light, the mist had settled. The things in it were larger now. Stronger. Stranger. They had staring white eyes and curving claws. They had hooves and whipping tails and teeth like icicles. They were free.

And now filled with power, they returned to the shadows. Ready.

Waiting.

17
The Horde

Van and Pebble staggered onto the Fox Den grounds.

The adult Collectors had left them behind ages ago, and Van and Pebble had already made one run through the forest that night. Now, exhausted, they scrambled up a small hillside and looked across the grounds.

The Fox Den was in chaos.

The giant reception tent was on fire. Smoke and strange-colored light filled the air. A pileup of luxury cars smashed together in the drive, honking at the fire trucks trying to swerve through. In the gardens, operagoers laughed and screamed and fought. Broken scenery covered the deserted stage.

"Where's my mom?" Van shouted, scanning the mess with rising panic.

"Where's my uncle?" Pebble shouted back.

"Where's Van?" shouted Barnavelt from Pebble's head. "Oh, there you are, Van! Now where's Pebble?"

"Should we split up?" Van whirled toward Pebble. "You could—"

But Pebble just raised one arm, pointing straight ahead.

In the wide, dark clearing across the grounds lurked a horde of Wish Eaters.

There were dozens. Hundreds. More than he'd ever counted in one place, even on the night when he'd freed several of them from the Hold. These Eaters were far larger than the ones he'd released. They were larger than any living animal he'd ever seen.

And the Collectors were racing toward them.

Van spotted Razor and Eyelet and Jack charging past the oblivious operagoers, straight toward the clearing. They were small black shapes with silver nets and flashing spears. They were hideously outnumbered.

"Meteors," said Pebble. "Hundreds of wishes at once . . ."

Dread and helplessness and too many questions coursed through Van, nearly knocking him off his tired feet. He searched the crowd again. Still no flash of emerald green. No sign that anyone else saw the Eaters, or the Collectors, or the awful battle that was clearly about to come. "Can't anyone see what's happening?"

Pebble gave her head one tense little shake. ". . . All kinds of things people don't notice."

They both stared at the distant clearing. The first group of Collectors had nearly reached it. Eaters crept out of the shadows, the full size of their bodies creeping into the light. "Come on!" Pebble started down the slope.

Van hurried after her. "What are we going to do?"

"I don't know!" Barnavelt called back from the top of Pebble's head. "What *are* we going to do?"

They scrambled through the mess of granted wishes. Van spotted a heap of gemstones with three men brawling beside it, the remains of a fallen grand piano, crates of lost baseball cards and teddy bears and books that no one had ever read.

Pebble had told Van long ago that people wished for stupid things. A grand piano and books and teddy bears weren't stupid—but what was truly stupid, Van realized, was the oblivious way the people around them were behaving, so caught up in their own wishes that they couldn't see the dangers swirling everywhere.

In the distance, the mass of Wish Eaters loomed larger and larger. The first line of Collectors readied their lances, shouting words to one another that Van couldn't hear. Van pushed his aching legs across the grass. And then, in the very edge of his vision, he caught a flash of emerald green.

Van whipped around.

Not far from the paths leading to the stage, his mother knelt on the ground. Mr. Grey hunched beside her. Between them, sprawled on the grass next to the broken shards of a lighting pole, was a third body.

Someone smaller. Someone who lay very, very still.

Guilt and terror pummeled Van like two fists. Oh no. Oh *no*. He swayed between the distant Collectors and the knot of huddled people.

No, no, no.

It was Peter. He was hurt. Maybe worse. And it was all because of what Van had done. If he had just explained to Peter—or if he had let him come along tonight, then maybe—

Maybe—

He took two faltering steps closer. Someone nearby was shouting something, but Van couldn't turn to listen. He couldn't see anything but the lifeless figure on the ground. He was halfway to it when someone yanked his arm so hard that it spun his body around.

"Van!" Pebble shouted into his face. *"LOOK OUT!"*

Van glanced back. He caught a flash of hooves. A body like a bison's. A mouth full of fangs.

One massive Eater was charging straight toward them.

Pebble lunged to the right, dragging Van along. They pelted across the grass, dodging pools of melting chocolate, a hailstorm of falling pearls.

The Eater lunged after them. Without looking back again, Van could feel it surging nearer. A wave of cold seemed to exhale from it, as if its body was an oven filled with ice instead of fire.

They raced into the far clearing.

Other Collectors whirled around them, each one fighting a mass of howling Eaters. Eyelet swung a spear. Two Holders lashed a net around one huge Eater while two more beasts barreled closer. Razor tore through a mass of fog with his twin hooks, fresh blood streaking his hands. And Van knew that Eaters didn't bleed.

"Tree!" shrieked Barnavelt.

Pebble yanked Van to the side. The trunk of a huge oak scraped Van's arm. In the dimness, they'd almost hit it. The Eater changed its course too, galloping around the tree's other side. It wheeled back toward them, drawing so close that Van could feel its cold mist on his skin.

Pebble dragged him around another tree. They raced back toward the center of the clearing. The Eater kept pace.

It was toying with them, Van realized. It was letting them tire themselves out, and then—

Then—

He skidded sideways, suddenly alone.

Pebble had let go of his arm.

Van spun to see Pebble tearing away in the opposite direction, Barnavelt's tail streaming behind. The Eater raced after them.

"Pebble!" Van screamed.

He couldn't even hear his own voice above his thudding heart. He was too far away to do anything but watch as the Eater ran Pebble down.

Just before the beast reached her, Pebble hit the ground.

She rolled into a ball, Barnavelt clinging to her shoulder. The Eater galloped straight over her, its momentum carrying it forward across the clearing.

Van pelted across the grass. "Pebble!" He dropped to his knees. "Are you okay?"

"What are you doing?" Pebble shouted back, unrolling herself. "That was your chance!"

"I'm not going to run away while you're all fighting a bunch of Eaters!"

"You're not one of us!" Pebble shot a glance across the clearing. The Eater had lumbered to a stop. Its massive head craned back toward them, its milky eyes fixing on them both. "Go!" she commanded. "Run somewhere safe!"

"No!" Van yelled. "I'm not leaving!"

"Yeah! We're not leaving!" echoed Barnavelt.

The bisonlike Eater broke into a run. It charged closer, huge head lowered, speed building.

Pebble grabbed Van by the arm once more. This time, she took off toward the edge of the clearing, heading for the thick fence of trees.

Van caught flashes of Collectors and Eaters as they ran: Jack's torn coat, Lemuel's black wings circling above, three Holders slashed by a lizard-shaped beast. Noise filled his ears like gritty mud. Pebble held tight to his arm, running even faster—

Until something bashed them to the ground.

Van's head thumped against the earth. One hearing aid tumbled out of place and vanished into the darkness. The air was crushed from his lungs. Icy cold crashed over him.

The Eater's hooves struck the ground inches from Van's skull. Van tucked himself into a ball and peered out through his arms. Beside him, Pebble was doing the same, her arms wrapped protectively around Barnavelt.

The Eater reared up onto its hind legs, its foggy body blotting out the stars.

Its hooves plunged down.

Before those hooves could crush them both, something slammed into the Eater's side.

The Eater toppled sideways. Its legs thrashed at the air. Snorting angrily, it heaved itself over and lurched back onto its hooves. It took a final look at Van and Pebble—or at something just above them—before lumbering away.

Van gazed up.

A ball of mist gazed back down at him.

It had wide, round, worried eyes. It had fuzzy ears, and a lemurlike tail, and a rounded body that had once fit in the palm of Van's hand, but that was now the size of a delivery truck.

"Lemmy?" Van breathed.

The Eater reached out with one long-fingered hand. Its fingertip, as delicate as dewdrops, touched Van on the cheek.

Van threw himself into the creature's arms.

The Wish Eater felt cool, soft, almost insubstantial, like cotton candy made from snow. Tiny beads of mist gathered on Van's skin as he hugged it tight.

Van leaned back, looking up into the creature's hubcap-sized eyes. "How did you even find me? Did you follow me all the way here from the city?" He recalled the swaying branches in the forest, the sense of something huge and hidden looming over him. "Have you been following me all this time?"

The Eater just gazed steadily back at him.

"Pebble, it's *Lemmy*!" Van spun toward her, beaming.

But Pebble's face was drawn and wary. Barnavelt crouched on her head, twitching skittishly.

"It helped us," Van prompted.

"Is it going to help us again?" asked Barnavelt.

"Again?" said Van. "What do you mean?"

"Again." The squirrel nodded past Van, toward the middle of the clearing.

The bisonlike Eater stood at a short distance, pawing the grass.

It lowered its massive head. Then, like a silvery battering ram, it charged.

Just as its icy cold crashed over them, Van's feet left the ground.

He was floating. No—he was *flying*. So was Pebble, with Barnavelt clinging to her shoulder. And so was Lemmy, who had lifted all of them straight up into the air.

Below, the charging Wish Eater skidded to a stop. Its massive body dwindled as Lemmy rose higher, other Eaters and Collectors around it shrinking into miniatures.

"Ha! You didn't get us, you big bully!" Barnavelt shrieked back toward the ground. "Bully bull! Bull bully! Bully bully bully . . ."

Lemmy turned toward the forest, and the clearing vanished from sight.

Treetops rustled below them. The starry sky arched above. Van smiled up at Lemmy, relief and joy so light in his chest that he felt like he could have flown on his own.

He glanced at Pebble. She wasn't smiling. Her hands clutched Lemmy's arm so hard that her knuckles glowed white.

Far from the clearing, Lemmy descended. It set Van and Pebble in the sturdy limbs of a big oak tree and hovered beside them, shielded by the canopy, like a cloud caught beneath a leafy umbrella. Barnavelt scurried happily into the branches.

"Thank you, Lemmy." Van reached out with one hand, holding tight to the tree with the other. The Eater bent its head to let Van rub its fuzzy ear. "You saved us twice."

Pebble stared at the Eater with an expression of distrust. Without speaking, she reached for the lower branches.

"Pebble," Van called. "What are you doing?"

With the leaves rustling around them, and with only one hearing aid, Van lost several of her words. ". . . back down there."

"You're going back down there? But—you can't! You don't even have a weapon. And there are too many Eaters. You'll be—"

". . . *have* to," Pebble cut him off. "This all may fall."

Fall? Van glanced at the sturdy branch beneath him. "Lemmy wouldn't—"

"She said, 'This is all my fault,'" Barnavelt put in, reappearing next to Van's hand. The squirrel tugged the cap off an acorn and began nibbling.

"It's not all your fault," Van called, before Pebble could climb any farther. "It's my fault too. We both helped bring the Collectors here. Maybe we can come up with a plan, or—"

". . . late for plans," said Pebble. "Any . . . not . . . stare . . . with an *Eater*."

And I'm not going to stay here with an Eater. Van glanced at Lemmy, who was still watching them with round, worried eyes. "This Eater just saved your life," he shot back.

"And other Eaters might be *killing my friends*!" Pebble shouted.

Another bolt of guilt and fear—this time, laced with love for Lemmy—shot through Van's insides. Between the Collectors and the other Eaters and the chaos at the Fox Den, how could they all possibly get out of this?

". . . understand." Pebble's voice was softer now. ". . . want to first."

"She said, 'I know you don't understand,'" said Barnavelt helpfully, through a mouthful of acorn. "'You're not one of us.'"

Van swayed on the branch. He caught himself with both hands, at the same moment that Lemmy gently reached out to prop him up. "Pebble, I'm on your side."

Pebble lunged back toward Van's branch, so he could see her face in the dim starlight. "You're not a *Collector*," she said. "You never will be. You weren't wished. You're not like us."

"But I can hear the Creatures," Van pleaded. "I can see you. And the Eaters."

"So can Uncle Ivor." Pebble's eyes were hard. "You're a normal person who *notices* things. And you think that makes those things yours. Just like him."

Her words cut Van in a raw, deep place. "I am *not* like him," he said, wishing his voice hadn't started to tremble. "Just because I can see both sides doesn't mean . . ."

But Pebble wasn't listening anymore.

She was staring into the distance, her eyes wide.

Van and Barnavelt and Lemmy looked too.

The sky above the Fox Den was filling with Wish Eaters. As they watched, more and more rose from the clearing, claws and tails and wings and paws massing together into a swirling silvery cloud.

Then, as one, the Wish Eaters streamed away—away from the Fox Den, away from the tree where Pebble and Van clung, staring after them. Soon they were only a faint trail of fog, and a moment later, they were nothing at all.

"Why are they leaving?" asked Van. "Where are they going?"

For a moment, Pebble didn't speak. Then she whirled toward Van, her face hard, her eyes on fire. *"We have to find my uncle. NOW."*

She scrambled down to the next branch.

"I'm coming!" Barnavelt called, stuffing the rest of the acorn into his mouth and bounding away.

"Wait," said Van, inching after the two of them. "We didn't see him at the Fox Den. Do you know where—"

Pebble's voice came through the leaves. "The *house*."

"But it will take us forever to get all the way back to your house!" Van turned to Lemmy. "Lemmy, you know where Mr. Falborg's house is, right?" The Wish Eater stared steadily at him. "Can you take us there?"

The Eater's eyes brightened. It scooped Van into one arm.

"Pebble," Van called as Lemmy floated past the branch where she clung. "Lemmy will take us straight to the house. Come on."

Pebble shot him a look that said she'd rather ride a giant tarantula made of poison ivy. She scrambled unsteadily for the next branch, muttering something that Van couldn't hear.

"What did she say?" Van asked Barnavelt.

"Oh. 'You can't trust an EATER,'" the squirrel answered cheerily, bouncing along the branch between them. "She also said, 'Are you crazy?' Do you want me to tell her yes or no?"

"Lemmy is *helping* us," Van insisted. "You saw it for yourself. Maybe Wish Eaters are only dangerous if people have been keeping them in boxes or cages for years and poking them with iron spikes."

Pebble didn't answer. Her sandals skidded on the next branch.

"It's going to take you half an hour to climb down *one tree*," said Van. "Aren't we in a hurry?" He leaned toward Pebble over Lemmy's misty arm. "I know you don't trust Eaters. But I trust *this* one. Don't you trust *me*?"

Finally Pebble halted. She turned toward Van, avoiding Lemmy's eyes. Her face was furious. "Fine," she muttered. ". . . Otherwise . . . too late."

Lemmy opened its free arm. Pebble edged along the branch toward it. She let the Wish Eater scoop her gently into the air, still not looking at its face. Her lips were pale and tight.

Barnavelt took a flying leap to Pebble's head.

"Wheeeeeee!" the squirrel crowed. "Let's go, let's go!"

Lemmy rose through the trees. It broke through the leafy canopy, and the night sky with its steadily burning stars surrounded them once more.

The Wish Eater steered toward the Falborg estate. As they skirted the Fox Den, Van caught the scent of smoke and the flash of red emergency lights. His thoughts shot to Peter, lying so still on the ground. His heart clenched. But he couldn't change what had happened. He could only try to stop things from getting even worse.

"Wheeee!" Barnavelt squealed again. "I've never climbed up this high before! Pebble, have you ever climbed up this high? Hey! Van! You're up here too! Isn't this great? Hey! Where are we going?"

The Wish Eater soared steadily ahead. Treetops rushed past their dangling feet. In minutes, the Falborg mansion appeared ahead of them, its peaked tower jutting through the woods.

Lemmy descended into a grove of pines at the edge of the Falborg lawn. Van and Pebble slipped out of the Eater's arms.

"Thank you, Lemmy." Van reached up to touch the Eater's dewy side.

"Yes," Pebble mumbled. "Thanks." She gazed at the Wish Eater for a moment, as though she might be about to say something else. But she whirled around and took off toward the house instead.

"She says, 'Hurry up, Van!'" the squirrel yelled from her shoulder.

"Lemmy." Van patted the Wish Eater's foot. "You should go. Hide somewhere safe. We don't want Mr. Falborg trying to re-collect you." He fought a sudden tightness in his throat. "But I hope . . . I hope I'll see you again."

Lemmy gave Van a shy smile before whisking off into the trees. In a blink, it was gone.

Van rushed to catch up with Pebble.

The brick mansion loomed before them, a still, sharp silhouette against the wavering darkness of the woods. Lights burned in the lower windows.

Pebble flung open the front door. "Uncle Ivor!" She stormed into the entry, Van tagging after. The light of the crystal chandeliers made him squint.

"Uncle Ivor!" Pebble yelled again. Her voice rang from the high ceiling. "Where are you?"

"Mabel?"

The voice wasn't Mr. Falborg's.

Van whipped around. Two figures emerged from a doorway to their left: a tall, broad-shouldered man with wavy gray hair and a woman in a neat linen suit.

Hans and Gerda.

Mr. Falborg's staff looked down at them with warm, surprised eyes.

"Why, Mabel," said Gerda, in the swooping accent that Van remembered. "*Look* achoo. What . . . all muddy . . . dis?"

"And Master Markson," said Hans, putting a big hand on Van's shoulder. "You look . . . all right?"

"He asked, 'Are you all right?'" prompted the squirrel on Pebble's shoulder. "Well, are you?"

Van's tongue went numb.

Hans and Gerda had always been kind to him. Of course, that was back when he was on Mr. Falborg's side. Did they know he was an enemy now?

"I . . . ," he began.

Pebble saved him by interrupting. "Where's Uncle Ivor?"

"Mr. Falborg . . . beck . . . opera yet," answered Gerda. "Come into the kitchen. . . . cleaned up. But Mabel . . ." She frowned at the squirrel on Pebble's shoulder. "I don't tink you should bring dat dirty rodent in here."

Without answering, Pebble dodged past Hans and Gerda. She plowed through the doorway where they'd emerged, Van once again racing to catch up.

"Mabel!" Gerda called after them. "What are you doing?"

"Did that woman call Van a dirty rodent?" Van heard Barnavelt ask. "That's not very nice."

Pebble rushed through a large, well-lit kitchen. A cup of steaming tea and an unfinished game of cards lay on the kitchen table. The air smelled faintly of cinnamon. Van wished he could plunk down in a padded chair, sip a cup of something warm, and play a lazy game of Go Fish—but the world of safe and comfortable things was falling apart around them. He wasn't sure that world would ever come back. Pebble hurried to the back of the kitchen, and Van hurried after her, with Gerda and Hans shuffling confusedly behind.

Inside a huge walk-in pantry, Pebble wrenched open a wooden door. A burst of cool air swirled through it. On the other side, Van made out a flight of stairs leading steeply downward.

The cold, stone-scented air sent Van's thoughts to the Collection, to that long staircase descending into the darkness. Pebble charged down the stairs ahead of him. She flicked on a light switch as she ran.

Van followed her into the mansion's basement.

The basement had high ceilings, stone walls, and several huge chambers branching off from a central room. Dusty lights glowed from the rafters. It was the kind of place where a very wealthy person might store thousands of bottles of wine, or build a hidden swimming pool, or install a giant pipe organ. Van had seen basements like this one beneath French châteaus. But Mr. Falborg's basement didn't have a wine cellar or a swimming pool or a pipe organ.

It had boxes. Empty boxes.

They were scattered across the stone floor, tumbling from shelves and spilling from every corner. Small cardboard boxes. Wooden chests. Brass-tacked steamer trunks. All of them were open, their lids gaping or tossed aside. And all of them were empty.

"Should've known . . . ," Pebble breathed, her words carrying through the still underground air.

"Known what?" asked Van, scurrying closer.

"All those Eaters at the Fox Den." Pebble gestured to the empty boxes, to the open doorways of the basement's other chambers. "They were *his*."

She pressed her hands to either side of her head. The

squirrel skittered out of the way of her fingers.

Pebble mumbled something that sounded like *All the pain . . .*

"What is she saying?" Van asked Barnavelt.

The squirrel blinked back at him. "Oh. She says it was all a plan. That Uncle Ivor knew about the meteor shower, and that there would be a big crowd at the opera for opening night. He must have had Hans and Gerda release the Eaters while he was at the Fox Den, so they could eat all the wishes that the crowd made and grow huge and powerful. Then he sent them away. And I know where they went. Wait." The squirrel blinked again. "*I* don't know where they went."

"I do." Van recalled the Wish Eaters dwindling into the distance. "They went to the city."

Pebble nodded. "To the *Collection.*" Now her voice was like ground glass. It sawed straight into Van's ears. "But the Holders are here. Because *I called them here.*"

"So the Hold will be unguarded," Van said, putting the rest of the pieces together. "Mr. Falborg's Eaters will swarm in and release all the other Eaters, and destroy the Collection, and then . . ."

Pebble finished for him. "He'll have an *army.*"

Van began to ask another question, but Pebble

suddenly froze. Her eyes went wide. Her head whipped toward the top of the stairs.

It was only then that Van realized something: Hans and Gerda hadn't followed them into the basement.

There was a thump as the basement door swung shut.

A look of fear and fury flashed across Pebble's face.

"What is it?" asked Van.

"I don't know," answered Barnavelt. "But I think I heard a click. Did I hear a click?" The squirrel paused for an instant, glancing from Pebble to Van. "Oh. That makes sense."

"What makes sense?"

Barnavelt's inky eyes stared at him. "Pebble says, 'They locked us in.'"

18
Blackout

"Gerda!" Pebble pounded at the basement door. *"Hans! Let us out!"*

Below her, Van turned in a slow circle. With one hearing aid gone, even Pebble's loudest yells sounded weak and mushy. There was no point in yelling for Hans and Gerda anyway. Mr. Falborg's assistants hadn't locked them in the basement by accident.

They would have to find another way out.

Van scanned their resources. Other than the heaps of empty boxes, the basement was empty. There were no tools for door smashing, no handy ladders for climbing up to the basement's high and narrow windows. There was nothing but bare stone walls, a hanging fuse box, and a bedraggled girl with a squirrel on her head stomping back down a staircase.

The squirrel's eyes landed on Van. "Hey! Van!" it squeaked cheerily. "You're locked down here too?"

"Barnavelt, those windows are too small for us," said Van. "But do you think *you* could get through?"

Barnavelt leaped from Pebble's head. In three jumps, he had bounded up the stone wall and reached one of the tiny windows. He nudged its frame outward.

"I can get through!" he announced. "Hey, this glass is really dirty. Now my paws are really dirty." The squirrel blinked down at them. "You know what? I don't think you two can fit through this window."

Van stepped closer. "But maybe *you* could run back to the Fox Den and tell the Collectors that we're trapped here."

"No," said a muffled voice.

Van turned.

Pebble had collapsed on the floor behind him. "No point," she said, her voice thick. "It's too late. And it's my fault."

Van hurried toward her, kneeling down to look into her face. Barnavelt jumped from the windowsill to Van's shoulder, taking the opportunity to wipe his dirty paws on Van's dress shirt.

"I was so *stupid*." Pebble's mossy eyes were wet. "Uncle Ivor tricked me. The wishing well, his plans—it was all pretend. It was just a way to get the Collectors here. I thought I was spying on him, being so clever and careful, but the whole time—" She choked, her voice breaking. "The whole time, he was just using me."

"You didn't know." Van put one hand on Pebble's back. She sagged beneath his touch, as though her body was shrinking into itself.

Pebble sobbed something Van couldn't catch.

"She says, 'I *should* have,'" Barnavelt murmured. "She says, 'He uses everybody. I just didn't think he'd do it to me. Not after everything.' She says, 'Everything is ruined, and it's my fault.'"

Van's chest ached.

The guilt he carried for hurting his mother, and now for injuring Peter too, was almost too much to lift. He could only imagine the weight crushing Pebble now.

He pressed his shoulder against hers. "We're still with you, Pebble," he said.

"Yeah," Barnavelt chimed in, hopping from Van's shoulder to hers. "I'd get trapped anywhere with you."

Pebble sniffled. Her head stayed bowed.

Van scanned the basement again, his eyes like razors.

There had to be *something* here. Could they bash the door with one of the old steamer trunks? Was there a hairpin or a lost nail somewhere that might help them try to pick the lock? His gaze slashed over something dull and unobtrusive hanging on the wall. Something that usually went unnoticed.

The fuse box.

Van had seen similar boxes backstage, in opera houses and theaters around the world. Lighting technicians were usually very nice to a small boy watching shyly from the wings. He'd helped them aim spotlights and change colored gels. Sometimes he'd even gotten to flip switches.

And suddenly, Van knew what to do.

Dread and hope spiked through him. He didn't like the dark. He didn't want to give up his vision—his sharpest sense, the tool that let him understand Pebble and that kept him from stumbling into danger. But he needed to take this chance.

"Pebble," he whispered. "Get ready. When Hans and Gerda come down here, we run."

Pebble's head lifted slightly. "But—"

Van wasn't about to waste time arguing. Jumping to his feet, he scurried to the box and opened its metal door. Two rows of horizontal switches waited inside. And at the bottom of those rows, twice as wide as the rest, was one big red switch.

The master.

Van pried the switch to the side.

It snapped down with a forceful click. The basement went black. In the same instant, Van felt something buzz to a stop in the walls and ceiling all around him— as though by flipping that switch, he had shut off the power in the entire huge house.

Because he had.

Van whirled back toward Pebble and Barnavelt. The glow of the narrow windows gave him just enough light to catch the glints of their eyes.

"What happened?" Barnavelt squeaked. "What time is it?"

In the dimness, Van grabbed Pebble's arm and pulled her close to the staircase. They huddled there, shoulder against shoulder.

The basement door inched open above.

"Mabel? Master Markson?" called Gerda's voice. "Half . . . play . . . the fuse box?"

Van held his breath. Beside him, Pebble and Barnavelt kept still.

Gerda and Hans muttered to each other in a language Van could barely hear and didn't understand anyway. They crept slowly down the stairs, their outlines blacker blots against the dark.

Hans stepped toward the fuse box.

At the same moment, Van yanked Pebble up the staircase.

Gerda shouted behind them, but Van and Pebble were already halfway up the steps.

Pebble slammed the door and turned the bolt.

Just in time.

The basement door rattled with the force of pounding fists. Muffled voices yelled.

"Ooh," murmured Barnavelt. "They're really angry."

"You can understand their language?" Van asked.

"No," Barnavelt answered. "But I understand angry."

Pebble grabbed a wooden chair and wedged it under the doorknob. Then, with a nod at Van, she raced toward the kitchen.

". . . should . . . time," she called back over her shoulder. "Just need . . . find out . . . Uncle Ivor's planning."

"But is Mr. Falborg even here?" Van asked, skidding across the kitchen's tile floor. "How do you know there's anything to find?"

"Why . . . basement. . . something?"

"Why what?" Van asked.

"She says, 'Why would Hans and Gerda lock us in the basement if they weren't protecting something?'" Barnavelt answered. "Ooh. That's a good point."

They dashed through the dark entryway. Van tried to look in every direction at once, expecting Mr. Falborg— or perhaps a monstrous Eater—to glide silently out of the shadows. But the only sign of life was their own footsteps making the floorboards tremble, their own quick breaths stirring the air.

At the entrance to the gigantic living room, they both skidded to a stop.

A row of suits of armor stood across the archway. Their metal gloves grasped axes, maces, heavy broadswords. Even in the dimness, the weapons glittered. If it weren't for the pedestals beneath them, and the fact that they stood inhumanly still, they would have looked like a row of knights standing guard.

"Were those there before?" asked Barnavelt softly. "Because I don't remember those being there before."

Van's eyes flicked past the suits of armor. Drifting toward the ceiling of the huge chamber was a burst of silvery mist.

A wish coming true.

". . . fit between them," said Pebble, in a way that made Van think she was coaching herself as much as him. Ducking her head beneath two knights' metal elbows, Pebble darted through the suits of armor into the next room.

It was just like squeezing through a big fence, Van told himself, crouching into the smallest shape possible. Keeping one eye on a glinting battle-ax, he inched past the hollow knights and into the next chamber.

Without the glow of its stained-glass lamps, the huge room felt unpleasantly dim and cold. Lumps of heavy furniture loomed through the dark. The dim, distorted blur of his own reflection slid across the glass display cases, making it look like someone else was creeping toward him.

Van's heartbeat staggered.

He hated this. He hated the darkness. He hated the way that it could hide the most dangerous secrets, no matter how carefully he looked.

"Van?" he thought he heard Pebble call. But he couldn't tell where the sound had come from, if it had come at all. He squinted through the shadows for the flutter of a white dress.

"Pebble?" he shouted. "Where are you?"

Behind him, a footfall made the floorboards vibrate. Van whirled around.

A suit of armor loomed over him. A beam of moonlight caught the ax in its—moving—hands.

"Van!" Barnavelt's voice yelled. "Over here! By the staircase!"

Van lunged away from the armor. He collided with an armchair, knocking it off its feet. Its fall shook the floor. Behind him, heavy footsteps drew closer. Van darted left, changing direction, tearing blindly through the shadows. His chest smacked the edge of a hard glass surface, knocking the air out of his lungs.

Van shoved himself backward from the display case. He dodged sideways, crashing into something warm and muddy. Something that smelled vaguely like flowers.

"Van!" squeaked Barnavelt's voice. "Where have *you* been?"

"Quick!" Pebble commanded, whirling away. ". . . the stairs!"

The pale splotch of her dress bounded up a wide wooden staircase. Van chased after it. He'd just reached the second step when a flash of metal streaked across his eyes.

The battle-ax smashed into the staircase. Wooden steps splintered. Shards flew and fell. Van staggered backward. The suit of armor hoisted its ax and brought it down again, obliterating the next stair.

It wasn't aiming at Van at all.

It was destroying the stairs.

Trapping Pebble above, and Van below.

Across the growing chasm, Van could see Pebble fling out her arms toward him, her open mouth shouting something he couldn't hear.

Van took one more backward step. Then he burst forward, leaping as high and as hard as he could. His feet wheeled over the missing stairs. Air rushed against his skin as the battle-ax swung behind him, its edge grazing the sole of one shoe.

He landed, off-balance and gasping, on the upper steps.

Pebble grabbed him with both hands. She hauled him to the top of the flight, not stopping to glance back until they were safe behind the banister of the upper hall. There, they both peered down into the huge chamber.

The suit of armor was still hacking at the staircase. If they needed to escape the house now, they would have to find some other way.

"He's using wishes," Van panted. "Mr. Falborg. To stop us."

"... keep us away," he thought he heard Pebble answer over another creak and smash. "Musty old house."

We must be getting close.

"Where do you think he is?" Van called as Pebble led the way into a hall lined with closed doors.

Her answer was lost in the pound of running feet.

"She says she has to get something,'" Barnavelt explained, turning around to face Van. "Hey! Van! Where have *you* been?"

Pebble threw open the door at the very end of the hall. Van slipped through after her. Enough moonlight filtered through the lace-curtained windows to reveal that they'd entered an ordinary bedroom.

An ordinary, very prissy, bedroom.

A canopy bed stood in its center, piled with a mound of china dolls. Van spotted a matching dresser and vanity, and a shelf lined with dancing porcelain girls in skirts that looked like upside-down tulips.

"Is this *your* room?" he asked wonderingly.

Pebble's head was buried in the closet. She whipped around, dragging something dark and lumpy out with her. "It's *Mabel's* room," she said.

She shook out the lumpy object. It was a coat—the same dingy, too large, full-of-pockets coat that Pebble had worn when Van first spotted her beside the fountain in the park. It was the coat that Pebble—the old Pebble, the *real* Pebble—had always worn.

She pulled it on, looking more like she was sinking into a warm bubble bath than into a lumpy piece of wool. The white sundress disappeared beneath it. Pebble stood up straighter. Her eyes glinted like pennies at the bottom of a fountain.

"That's better," she murmured.

"Much better," agreed Barnavelt, rubbing his head against its dingy collar.

Pebble patted the coat's many pockets, as if checking for objects she already knew would be there. From one of the large inner pockets, she pulled out a flashlight and clicked it on.

"There," she said, tilting the flashlight so that Van could see her mouth. Her eyes glittered in its beam. "*Now* we find my uncle."

They ran back along the corridor. Pebble's stride was straighter and stronger than before, which made Van's straighter and stronger too. They charged along, the flashlight's beam slicing the dark ahead of them, until

Pebble veered into the hallway crammed with kites.

Pebble muttered something under her breath.

"What did she say?" Van asked.

"A rude word," whispered Barnavelt, awed.

"Why?"

"She said she didn't mean to take this route, but—"

A bird-shaped kite dove from the ceiling.

Barnavelt broke off with a squeak. The kite flew at Pebble, its string unraveling behind it. Pebble ducked, but the kite ducked with her, circling, its string forming a tightening loop around her limbs.

Before she could break free, another kite swooped down. Then a dozen. Then more.

Three paper kites whipped past Van's neck. He threw up his hands protectively, and the kites' edges slashed burning trails across his palms. Tangling strings and kite tails wrapped around him. The harder he fought, the harder the kites whirled, more and more of them joining the bright cyclone that spun around him. Rope burns and paper cuts crisscrossed his arms.

"Pebble!" he called.

But there was no answer that he could catch—just the flash of her light hitting the floor, its beam streaking across the walls before going still.

Van squinted through the whirling kites.

A few steps away, Pebble writhed in a tornado of kites, her body wrapped like a bug in spiders' thread. Barnavelt ran frenziedly back and forth across her shoulders.

"Barnavelt!" Van yelled, wriggling one hand through the strings that tightened around his neck. "Use your teeth!"

"I already tried!" the squirrel shouted back. "Kites don't care if you bite them!"

Van slapped two kites aside with his freed hand. "Use your teeth *on the strings*!"

"Oh!" Barnavelt dove toward Pebble's neck. With three rapid bites, he gnawed through the mass of strings.

Pebble thrust her arms upward. Fibers popped as she pushed and thrashed, shoving the knots down to her ankles. Barnavelt lunged from her shoulders to Van's, biting at his strings until Van was free too. Kicking off the heaps of thread, the three of them pelted to the end of the hall, Pebble snatching up the flashlight as they ran.

They skidded through a heavy door. Van slammed it shut behind them, following Pebble's light down yet another corridor. Pebble shouted something over her shoulder—something with the words "safe" and "fast" tangled in it. But Van suspected that they wouldn't be *safe* anywhere.

Mr. Falborg wasn't just using wishes to keep them away. Intentionally or accidentally, his wishes were trying to hurt them. Or to stop them for good.

They ran past a ballroom with a parquet floor gleaming like black ice, and a high-ceilinged gallery of paintings that shone like oil slicks in the moonlight. They passed dim rooms with open doors, where shadow boxes full of trinkets glittered softly. In one room, Van caught sight of a case filled with what looked like superhero figurines. He halted for a split second, one foot wanting to step inside and look closer, the other trying to carry him onward. With a stumble, he turned back to the hallway.

But the glow of Pebble's flashlight had disappeared.

"Pebble?" he called. "Barnavelt?"

Ahead of him, the hallway bent to the right. Van followed it, jogging into a corridor so dark that he couldn't make out the walls or floor. There were no windows. And there was no beam of light. He reached for the wall and found the wood of a closed door instead. Next to it was another door, and another, and another, all of them shut.

"Pebble?" he called again.

There was no reply.

Van's heart tripped.

If Pebble had just run ahead of him down the hallway, he would have caught sight of the flashlight somewhere in the distance. But it had vanished. Pebble must have stepped through one of these doors. But which one?

Van fumbled for the knob of the nearest door.

The room inside was like a library—but vinyl records, not books, stuffed its floor-to-ceiling shelves. Tall, narrow windows let in enough light to assure him that no one was there. Van groped along the hall to the next doorway. Inside, rows of tiny glass windows winked back at him. Dollhouses, Van realized. Dozens of them. Through their open sides, he peeped into miniature dining rooms and kitchens, at tables set with dime-sized plates and silverware no longer than a staple. They reminded him of his own model stage. For a moment, Van pictured Mr. Falborg carefully arranging these miniatures, decorating the tiny, cozy rooms that no one else would ever touch or see.

I'm not like that, Van told himself. He thought of the leaf in amber that he'd passed to Peter, and the twinkly marble he'd given Pebble to keep. *I'm not.* Still, a sad, sick feeling followed him onward, down the hall.

The third room held a collection of seashells, but no Pebble. The fourth had racks of antique medicine bottles, but no Pebble. More than once, Van groped for a light switch, remembering too late that the switches wouldn't help. Hans and Gerda had obviously decided to leave the power off and let them stumble around in the dark. Knowing that there would be no light if he needed it— he didn't even know where to search for a flashlight or a match—made the sick feeling worse. His breath came in tight, high wheezes. Every shift in the air made him jump.

He was just edging back into the hall when he heard a sound.

Van stopped, listening.

He couldn't tell where it had come from or what it had said, but it sounded like a voice.

Pulling his courage tight around himself, he hurried forward.

The voice spoke again. Van turned his head, trying to catch it. It *was* a voice. It was calling something. Something that sounded like ". . . Here!"

"Hello?" Van called back.

"Here!" the voice yelled again.

He must have been drawing closer, because the voice seemed clearer now. And it definitely sounded like Pebble.

Van grasped the knob of the last door in the hall.

"Pebble?" he called into the opening doorway.

"Over here!"

The room beyond the door was dark and cavernous. Van could feel its size in the stillness of the air. Faint moonlight outlined the edges of its thick velvet curtains. As he inched inside, hands extended in front of him, his fingers struck the edges of hard wooden surfaces, scattered bits of furniture filling the floor.

"Mabel," called a gentle voice.

Van froze.

This voice was too deep to be Pebble's. It couldn't have belonged to Hans or Gerda—they were still trapped downstairs, as far as he knew. There was only one other person in this vast house that the voice could belong to.

Van squinted into the darkness. He couldn't make out where Mr. Falborg stood. But the voice had to have come from within this room.

He wasn't going to face Mr. Falborg in the dark. With a burst of panic, Van raced across the room, bumping tables and shelves as he ran. He ripped the velvet curtains aside.

Blue light filled the room.

Mr. Falborg wasn't there.

Panting, Van scanned his surroundings. The room where he stood was large, but so cluttered that it was hard to feel its space at all. Every inch was crammed with strange wooden contraptions, some of them small enough to fit in a palm, others as large as a wedding cake, and some larger still—the size of wardrobes or grandfather clocks. Wires and cogs and other odd brass parts gleamed in the moonlight.

This was Mr. Falborg's music box collection.

On the table nearest Van was something that looked like a huge metal morning glory. Its stem sprouted from a wooden box. As Van watched, a cylinder on the box began to spin.

"Mabel," called Mr. Falborg's voice. "Mabel. Mabel."

Van grabbed the spinning cylinder. The voice stopped. Stillness filled the room.

Relief, and then a fresh wave of worry, swept through Van. Was this all a trick? What was going on?

"Over here!" called Pebble's voice from somewhere in the darkness.

Van's heart lifted. But with only one hearing aid, it was harder than ever to tell where the voice had come from.

"Pebble?" he shouted back.

He scanned the jumbled furniture. Was Pebble hidden behind a shelf? Was she trapped in a big wooden cabinet? Where else could she be?

From close by, Mr. Falborg's voice spoke again.

"Mabel . . ."

Van whipped around. The machine had turned itself back on. As Van stared, its cylinder spun faster and faster, the name smearing into a chant. "Mabel. Mabelmabelmabel . . ."

Before Van could grab the cylinder, another sound stopped him. It was a loud, clanging, tinny sound— the sound of a very old music box playing a waltz. A machine to Van's left clicked into motion, its black disk spinning, and a soprano's voice pealed through the room. There was a blast of what might have been trumpets. Van thought he caught the blare of organ pipes. Then, one after another, every music box in the room burst to life.

Disks whirled. Keys clacked. Noise thickened in the air, leaving nothing for Van to breathe. He stumbled toward the door, feeling like he was balanced on a high ledge, with rain and wind battering him from every side.

A banging, thumping sound joined the storm. Van couldn't tell where it came from, whether it was one of the machines or something else entirely. But it was forceful enough that he could feel it shaking the floor.

He tried to focus on that feeling. But the music blared louder. The thumping came faster. Noise crammed his head until his skull ached.

Van stumbled to the doorway. He was about to plunge back into the dark hallway, leaving the noise behind, when he heard the scream.

Its frequency snagged Van like a line of razor wire. It was too clear and sharp to have come from a machine. This was the sound of something in pain. Something real. Something that reached straight inside of him.

Van rushed back into the room.

He tugged handles out of cranks. He slammed the lids of tinkling music boxes. He shoved one jangling contraption to the floor, where it smashed to splinters.

But he'd already lost the scream. The noise had knocked him off course.

"Over here!" called Pebble's voice.

The *recording* of Pebble's voice.

How hadn't he noticed before? The voice wasn't real. It had never been real. It was only another trick.

Furious now, Van crashed through a row of tall cabinets, lunging into a corner where another metal morning glory sat on a velvet-draped table. A vinyl record spun beneath it.

"Over—" said Pebble.

Van ripped the record from under the needle. Pebble's voice slurred and vanished. He hurled the record across the room, where it hit the wall and shattered.

Van stood, breathing hard, using the scraps of all his senses. He ignored the spinning disks and moving keys, all the things that didn't matter. He waited. And then, just below him, in the shadows where the moonlight couldn't reach, his eyes caught a tiny twitch. The twitch of something alive.

Van dropped to his knees. He swept his palms across the floor. His hand struck something that moved. He patted cautiously at its edges, squinting through the dimness. It didn't feel like a music box. It had a flat wooden base with metal parts bolted to it, and when Van touched its side, he found a row of sharp, jagged teeth.

It was a rattrap. A large one.

And pinned between its jagged teeth and its metal arm, blood dulling his silvery fur, was Barnavelt.

The squirrel had followed Pebble's voice too.

19
Trapped

Van's heart slid into his stomach.

"Barnavelt." He leaned close. "Can you hear me?"

For once, the squirrel kept silent.

As gently as he could, Van tugged the trap across the floor, into a beam of moonlight.

Barnavelt's eyes were closed. Shivers shook his body. The trap's metal teeth had caught him on one side, at the top of a rear leg. A gleaming black trail of blood marked the trap's path across the floor.

Van's heart and stomach plummeted toward his shoes. He patted desperately at the metal rod, but he couldn't find a button to release it. He couldn't risk prying it open only to have it spring shut again. He was so focused on the trap that for a while he couldn't hear the voice shouting his name.

"VAN!" the voice bellowed. "VAN!"

Van listened. This voice wasn't a recording. It wasn't even coming from inside this room.

As the last few music boxes wound to a stop, he heard it again.

"VAN!" it screamed. "VAN, GET ME OUT OF HERE!"

Pebble.

Like he was lifting a piece of blown glass, Van settled the trapped squirrel against his chest. Warm splotches of blood seeped through the front of his dress shirt.

The thumping sound grew clearer as he hurried out into the hall. Pebble's yells grew clearer too.

"VAN! *GET ME OUT!*"

The door across the hall shivered in its frame.

Van grabbed the knob and wrenched it sideways. The door flew open.

". . . didn't even . . . shut and locked behind me!" Pebble shouted, bursting out into the hall. "I've been shouting and shouting, and—"

Her eyes flicked to the object pressed to Van's chest. Something terrible passed over her face. "What . . ."

"Barnavelt," Van managed. "In a rattrap."

Pebble dragged them into a room lined with tall

windows. Shelves crammed with antique toys stood all around them, motionless animals and untouched dolls staring blankly down.

Van set Barnavelt on the floor before the windows. The only sound Barnavelt made was a tiny, breathy whimper, so thin that Van could barely hear it.

". . . Hold the sides?" asked Pebble, in a voice that sounded like she had swallowed something sharp.

Van steadied the trap with both hands. Delicately, Pebble wormed her fingers under the metal bar and pried it back.

Barnavelt didn't move. Even his shivering had stopped.

Pebble lifted him from the trap's metal teeth. His body lay limp in her hands, small droplets dribbling from his back paw.

Pebble cradled Barnavelt to her chest. She bowed her head, enclosing him between her arm and chin, as though he might slip away. She mumbled something. The only words Van caught were *Uncle Ivor*. The look on her face told him everything else.

Van wanted to comfort her, even if he didn't believe his own words. "Maybe Mr. Falborg didn't try to hurt him. Maybe it was an accident. A wish gone wrong."

Pebble didn't answer. She just looked at Van, her eyes like two small fires.

Abruptly, she patted at her coat's many pockets. "Maybe . . . bandage," he heard her mutter. She tossed the contents of the pockets to the floor. A tiny folding knife. A spare battery. A wishbone in a paper napkin. Her hand shook. ". . . make a splint . . . string . . ."

"Pebble," said Van. "He needs a lot more than a splint."

He reached for the wishbone on the floor.

"What . . .?" whispered Pebble. ". . . know how dangerous it can be!"

"Sometimes you have to take the risk. Like you said."

Van stood and unlatched the nearest window. A gust of cool, piney air swept inside.

"Van." Now Pebble's voice was half choked by a sob. "I can't risk *Barnavelt*."

"But if we don't do something fast, he might not make it."

Both of them looked at the squirrel curled, motionless, against Pebble's chest. Neither of them needed to remind the other that wishes couldn't bring things back from the dead.

Van craned out the window, holding the wishbone

in his fingertips. Hope faltered in his chest. Maybe this wouldn't work either. Maybe his plan would fail before it had begun. But then, amid the trees, a patch of white mist glimmered closer.

A moment later, Lemmy's cloudy body filled the window, its wide eyes glancing from the wishbone to Van's face.

"Come in, Lemmy," Van whispered.

Lemmy floated over the windowsill. Its eyes fell on Pebble and the bundle in her arms.

Pebble held the squirrel closer.

Van knelt beside her. "It will be okay," he said softly, grasping the ends of the wishbone. "Lemmy will help us."

"Wait." Pebble raised her head. She looked into Van's eyes. Up close, he could follow her lips and catch each word. "Maybe you should wish for something else."

"What?"

"You should wish . . ." She swallowed. "You should wish for both you and Barnavelt to get out of here."

"What?" said Van again. "No."

"Van," Pebble insisted. "You don't need to do this. You can get out. Go find your mom. Be safe."

"No," said Van. "I'm not leaving you."

Pebble went quiet. Her fingers stroked Barnavelt's fur.

"Maybe we should use the wish for something even bigger," said Van. "It is the only one we have."

"Like . . . stopping my uncle?"

Van nodded.

"But the bigger the wish, the more can go wrong. And if Barnavelt doesn't . . . if he isn't—" Pebble broke off, swallowing again. "Barnavelt needs it most. I'll have to stop my uncle by myself."

"You mean *we'll* stop him," said Van.

Pebble met his eyes once more. "*We* will." She took a deep breath, grasping one end of the wishbone. "Okay. Go ahead."

Van grasped the bone's other end. *I wish for Barnavelt to be all right,* he thought, as clearly and forcefully as he could.

The bone snapped. Pale droplets fell from Van's broken half, drifting down as lightly as soap bubbles.

The Wish Eater bent to swallow them.

A burst of mist surged through the room. Dew collected on Van's eyelashes, gathering on the strands of his hair. He took a breath, feeling its magic *whoosh* into his body and float out again.

In Pebble's arms, Barnavelt stirred. He rolled over, revealing a wound where the blood had begun to clot at last. His inky eyes opened.

"Pebble?" he asked drowsily, blinking up at her. "Hey! Where have you been?"

Pebble let out a laugh-sob.

"Good job, Lemmy," Van breathed.

Everyone kept quiet for a moment—even Barnavelt, wrapped in Pebble's arms.

Then, very slowly, the Wish Eater held out its hands. It hovered next to Pebble, waiting.

Pebble glanced up. Instinctively, she recoiled, pulling Barnavelt away.

Van watched Pebble cower, and he watched Lemmy wait with its long-fingered hands open, and he understood what had to happen next.

"Pebble," he murmured. "This is how Barnavelt will be all right. Lemmy will get him out and keep him safe. This is how the wish comes true."

Pebble hesitated for another long beat. She looked at Van, her fingers stroking anxiously at Barnavelt's fur. Then she turned her eyes to Lemmy. The Eater gazed back at her. Its eyes were bright and steady.

Something inside Pebble seemed to release. Her

tensed arm opened. Slowly, gently, she placed Barnavelt in Lemmy's hands.

"Keep him safe," she whispered. "I . . . I'm trusting you."

Lemmy tucked the squirrel into the curve of one misty arm.

"Hey," murmured Barnavelt in a sleepy voice. "I'm flying again. I'm flying in a big pillow. Hey, Pebble. Do you see me flying?"

Lemmy squeezed through the open window frame. The Eater floated out into the night, carrying Barnavelt with it.

Pebble watched until they had vanished into the trees. She spun back toward Van so suddenly that Van jumped.

"Now we find my uncle," she said.

Then she bolted for the door.

20
Time to Choose

They stormed through the fourth floor, flinging open doors, bolting down empty hallways. There was no trace of Mr. Falborg himself, although signs of his obsessions were everywhere: framed stamps and marble statues, puppets and matchbooks, shields and teacups, coins and bones; thousands—millions—of precious things that now belonged to one person alone. And here they were, shut up in an echoing old house, where no one else would ever glimpse them.

The more he saw, the sicker Van felt.

"Fifth floor," Pebble called over her shoulder.

They rushed up a narrow staircase.

It led them to a round chamber where a collection of antique tapestries covered the walls. They had reached the tower at the end of the house, Van realized. A spiral staircase wound up through the ceiling. Small windows let in slips of dark sky. From the corner of his eye, Van saw something streak past those windows—something silvery and large, lit by a red-gold glow.

They raced upward. The stairs twisted beneath them, making turn after turn. Van's heart pounded harder. His knees grew wobblier. From above, he could feel the shift of moving air, a breeze that was dewy and scented with pine. They ran until at last they reached the final step and staggered out onto a wide wooden floor.

They had reached the top of the tower. The peaked metal ceiling thrust upward above them. In the center of the room stood a towering glass case filled with bottles—bottles that pulsed with a reddish, smoldering light. Large windows encircled the whole chamber, letting in a haze of night sky. And standing in front of one open window, his back to them, his white suit glowing with reflected light, was Ivor Falborg.

Mr. Falborg closed the window. The cool breeze died. The room turned echoingly quiet. Mr. Falborg turned to face Van and Pebble, cupping a last smoldering bottle in both hands.

"Ah, Mabel. And Master Markson." Mr. Falborg smiled, his crinkly blue eyes landing on the two of them without a hint of surprise. The room was still enough, and the glow bright enough, that Van managed to follow his words. "Well, this is wonderfully convenient timing. We've just finished our work."

Van saw Pebble suck in a breath. Her eyes were wide. Furious. Horrified.

"The dead wishes." She inched forward like an animal on a leash. Van crept forward too, keeping her face in sight. "*That's* what you wanted."

"Of course." Mr. Falborg raised the glowing glass bottle in his hands. Still smiling, he nodded toward the windows. "And I've had wonderful assistance."

Van followed his gaze. The swarm of Wish Eaters had gathered just outside the windows, their moonlight-tinged bodies forming a silvery mass around the tower. They drifted past the windowpanes, teeth glinting, pale eyes staring in, like sharks in a backward aquarium. The back of Van's arms pricked with fear.

"That's why you did all of this." Pebble's voice was flat, not questioning, but setting out the facts. Van wondered if, deep down, she still hoped Mr. Falborg would argue with them. "You tricked me into luring the Holders here, so your Eaters could steal the dead wishes and bring them back to you."

"Exactly," said Mr. Falborg, as though Pebble had just recited the steps to a cookie recipe. "Wish Eaters are extremely loyal. Once you've fed and protected them, they're yours for life." His twinkly eyes moved to Van. "You've learned that firsthand, haven't you, Master Markson?"

Van started. "I . . . But—Lemmy isn't *mine*. It came back to me because it wanted to."

"Do you see any cages around these creatures?" asked Mr. Falborg, gesturing to the swarm outside. "Any nets or cruel iron prods, as are used by your Collectors?" His eyes flicked to the lance in Pebble's hand. "These wonderful beings are mine by choice. They know that I will provide for them."

"Is that what you're going to do with the dead wishes?" Pebble cut in, her voice flatter and harder than before. "Feed them to your Eaters?"

"Of course not." Mr. Falborg brushed the lapel of his white suit, as though he was shooing away imaginary dirt. "At least, not all at once."

"But—"

Mr. Falborg raised a hand, cutting Pebble off. "I am

aware of their power. I honor that power. That's why I am the right person to keep them."

"What makes you think you're right at all?" Van blurted, before he could help it. "You lie. You trick people. You use people to get the things you want."

Mr. Falborg's eyebrows rose. "Haven't you done the same, Master Markson?" He stepped close to Van, bending down to speak straight into Van's face. The glow of the dead wish glittered in his eyes. "Think of how you've used the people around you. Think of how often you've lied to your lovely mother. Think of the secrets you kept from Pebble and the Collectors and poor Peter Grey."

"But . . . I *had* to!" Van protested.

"Yes, you did," agreed Mr. Falborg. "You knew you were acting for the greater good. You wanted to save something larger than yourself. That is what I do as well. I am a collector." His eyes shifted to Pebble. "Not a prison guard. Not a torturer. Not a thief of other people's wishes."

"But you hurt us," said Pebble. Her voice started low, growing louder and louder until it rang from the stone walls. "You almost crushed Van with a train. Your Eater nearly trampled us. Your stupid trap almost *killed Barnavelt*!"

"Incidental," said Mr. Falborg, the way someone else might have said "A mere drizzle." He shook his head apologetically. "I am sorry to have given you such a fright. But everything has turned out for the best, hasn't it?" Mr. Falborg straightened, holding the dead wish between them like a bomb with a lit fuse. "Which gives us the perfect chance for a fresh start."

As he went on, Mr. Falborg stepped toward a window, angling his face away. Van lost most of his next words. He thought he caught "children" and "mistakes" and "understand"—but then Mr. Falborg unlatched the window, letting in a fresh gust of air, and turned back to them, drawing a wishbone from his vest pocket.

Van's heart went still.

Mr. Falborg couldn't kill them with a wish. But he could do something pretty close. And there was no safe way to stop him, not while he held that dead wish in his other hand.

"Where shall we begin?" Mr. Falborg asked. "Perhaps with Mabel?" His eyes settled on her, gentle and warm. "Mabel," he said softly. "I will forgive . . . betrayals . . . stay with me for good. This will be my wish for you: You will never see any of the Collectors or their Creatures again."

Pebble took a choking breath. The flashlight fell from her hand. The Eaters outside the window pressed close to the frame.

Mr. Falborg turned his gaze on Van. "Or shall we start with Master Markson?" Van stepped forward, his eyes trained on Mr. Falborg's face. "My wish for you," Mr. Falborg continued, "will be that you forget all of this. Everything you've seen. Everyone you've known. You will return to your own life, content and safe, perhaps with a new father and brother, without any memory of the trouble you've caused." Mr. Falborg gave him a tender smile. "You are not a Collector, Van Markson. You will never be one of them. And with their cruelty, why would you want to be?"

Van turned toward Pebble. His throat felt like it was being crushed in a gigantic fist. "He's right. He should start with me." He forced out the words. "We can't let Mr. Falborg keep you prisoner again. Besides, the Collectors need you, and I'm—I'm not really a Collector. I won't ever really be a Collector. You've said so yourself."

Pebble grabbed Van's hand. *"No,"* she said, squeezing tightly. She pulled him close. "You can't forget us. Maybe you're not exactly like us—but we need you too. *I* need you."

"Why?"

"*Because,*" said Pebble, her wide eyes staring into his. "Because you can see both sides. You see the good and the bad about Eaters and wishes and everything else. Because—you're *you.*"

Van glanced back at Mr. Falborg. The man in the white suit had gripped the ends of the wishbone and raised it toward the open window. Outside, the Eaters roared.

Both sides, Van thought. The good and the bad.

He'd discovered so much magic hidden in the world around him. The magic of wishes and Wish Eaters, the magic of Collectors and of ordinary people. That magic was both dangerous and wonderful—too dangerous and too wonderful for anyone, no matter their reasons, to control all of it. No one should be allowed to steal that power.

And no one was going to steal the power inside of him.

"Maybe we can stop this." Van turned to Pebble's mossy-penny eyes. "We have to try."

Pebble's eyes flared. She squeezed Van's hand once more. "*Together.*"

"I am sorry, dear Mabel," said Mr. Falborg. The bone in his grip began to bend.

Pebble charged forward. "My name is *PEBBLE*!" Van heard her scream.

Still holding tight to his friend's hand, Van charged too.

They flew at Mr. Falborg.

Pebble's shoulder struck him in the stomach. Mr. Falborg doubled over and quickly thrashed back, trying to raise the wishbone out of reach. But Van had already caught his arm. He clung to Mr. Falborg's elbow, one hand scrabbling for the bone, while Pebble wrenched at Mr. Falborg's other arm. Van's fingers closed around the wishbone's end. Mr. Falborg reached to stop him with the other hand—and in a moment so simultaneously fast and slow that Van couldn't stop it, even as he watched it unfold, Mr. Falborg lost his grip on the glowing bottle.

The falling wish flared. The glass shattered against the floor.

A blast filled the tower room.

A sound like the hum of ten thousand voices flooded the air, eating every wisp of oxygen. It rang in Van's skull and buzzed in his lungs. Wind ripped at his hair. The air turned the color of the heart of a fire—a white gold so bright that it burns without touching.

Just before the whirling light knocked them all to their knees, Van ripped the wishbone from Mr. Falborg's grasp.

The blast grew brighter, the sound swelling.

Van peered toward the spot where Pebble should have been. Everything was a blur. All he could see was the glow of the dead wishes in their glass case, burning red against the white gold, and the smear of the open window where the storm of Eaters was about to push its way inside.

Inside—to the released dead wish.

Van grasped the ends of the wishbone. He couldn't focus on a clear, simple wish. He could only remember a crowd of faces: Pebble, Barnavelt, Lemmy, Nail and Razor and Eyelet and Sesame and Jack, Charles and Peter Grey, even Mr. Falborg. And his mother, smiling down at him. All the good and all the bad, and everything in between. He could only hope, with every exhausted, terrified cell inside of him, that everyone would be all right.

The wishbone snapped. A fragile wisp whirled away on the fiery air.

There was a roaring, screeching, rending sound—and then the cold and the mist poured in.

21
Out of the Well

The thing at the bottom of the well was no longer asleep.

Noise had woken it. Strange noise, strange light, bursts of something that flavored the air.

Wishes, it realized, as their traces drifted over the trees and down into the dark. More wishes than it had ever sensed all at once.

Even wishes hardly interested the thing at the bottom of the well. It was old enough that hunger and want had burned to ashes long ago. It had ignored the silly little wishes of the black-coated ones, meant to lure it out. It hadn't survived for centuries by trusting every trap.

But the power it felt now was different. This was

something vast. Something strange. Something that had broken its rest, at the very least.

Sleepily, slowly, it dragged itself through its tunnels, its vast body sliding up the shaft of the well and drifting out into the night.

It ascended over the forest. Its body cast a shadow over the trees as it flew, like a cloud passing between the earth and the moon. The cool of the wind brushed its limbs.

From high above, unseen, it gazed down at the mess of the Fox Den, the tiny people scurrying below. It veered away from the mess of ordinary wishes, following the tug of that stronger power back over the woods, toward a rambling brick house with a peaked tower.

Other, smaller Eaters gathered here, whipping past the windows of that tower, where a reddish glow burned against the night. The thing from the bottom of the well glided lower. It sensed the power of the dead wishes collected inside, smoldering like a spark about to ignite a forest fire. A fire that would bring more feet trampling through its quiet woods, more noise and more trouble to the spot where it had slept in peaceful dimness for so long.

That spark needed to be put out.

The thing from the bottom of the well dove toward the tower. The other Eaters scattered around it like dry leaves. It grasped the peaked rooftop. With one clawed hand, it lifted off the metal roof and gazed down into the chamber below.

What it saw was a room blazing with wish magic. It saw the case crammed with burning, waiting wishes. It saw danger and destruction and fire and noise. It saw three tiny people, nearly crushed by the force around them. And it saw the smallest of them—a boy with wide eyes and black hair—looking back.

What the boy saw was a face: a face so large that it filled the hole where the roof had been. It was shifting and silvery, with a muzzle like a lion's. Pale whiskers whipped around its jaws. Its massive eyes were gray, as deep and reflective as ponds. Staring into them, the boy thought, was like staring into the eye of a blue whale, or into the heart of a redwood tree. It was something so large and so deep and so old that it made everything else on earth seem small.

The boy and the thing gazed at each other. The thing from the bottom of the well hadn't been seen in lifetimes. And with those ancient silver eyes on him, the boy knew he had never been seen this way before.

He wondered if he'd ever truly been seen at all.

Almost delicately, the thing from the bottom of the well reached one clawed hand into the tower. Bricks slipped and rained from the ceiling. The tower swayed. Without any effort, the thing crushed the glass case filled with dead wishes beneath its hand.

The light in the tower had been bright before. Now it was so searing that the people threw themselves to the floor. The thing from the bottom of the well watched them scuttle, panicked, against the walls, wrapping their arms over their heads. A blazing hum ripped the air.

The thing from the bottom of the well opened its mouth. It pulled in those thousands of dead wishes. It pulled in their noise and their fire and their force. It pulled in the faint wisp of one living wish, almost lost in the searing storm.

The massive Eater surged with power. The power to create. To destroy. To do anything it wished.

The thing from the bottom of the well had never gotten to make a wish of its own. And now, what it wished for was . . .

Quiet.

Beneath it, the swaying tower steadied. The wind died.

The swarm of Eaters backed away. One by one, and then in a receding tide, they flew off in all directions, scattering into the darkness.

Quiet rippled over the woods. It seeped through the grounds of the Fox Den, where fires flickered out, fights ended, and people sagged sleepily onto the grass. Jewelry and limousines disappeared in puffs of fog. Sirens died. Bones healed.

The thing from the bottom of the well took a last glance into the tower. The three people had gone still, huddled amid shards of glass and rubble. All that remained of the dead wishes was those sparkling shards, and a scorched spot on the floor.

The thing lifted back into the air.

It soared, a bit more heavily now, over the treetops to its silent clearing. It dragged its even more massive body down the shaft of the well. It slid legs and arms and winding tail into the underground tunnels where they belonged. It buried its claws in the cool earth. With a deep sigh, resting its chin on the ground, it gazed out at the pile of coins, glinting in the faint hints of starlight.

Then it closed its ancient eyes and settled down to sleep.

22
Quiet

Van and Pebble raised their heads.

The tower room was still. Brick dust spiraled slowly in the air, dancing with the last wisps of fog. Soft night wind shushed across the open roof above.

They wobbled to their feet. Van's hand still clutched the bits of a broken wishbone. Pebble's hand, he noticed, was closed around a swirling glass marble. They both slid the objects into their pockets.

"Is it gone?" Pebble asked, at the same moment that Van said, "Is it over?"

They froze, listening and looking. The window showed nothing but the dark forest outside. There were no whirling Wish Eaters. No screams. No sirens.

Pebble's eyes trailed across the room, landing on

a shape slumped against the wall. She bolted toward it. Van stumbled after her, his shoes skidding on the shards of broken glass.

Ivor Falborg lay in a heap of rubble. Bricks tumbled around him, their darkness eclipsing his white suit. One open hand was flung out on the stone floor before him, as though he were reaching for something that was no longer there.

Pebble put her ear to his lips.

". . . Alive," she said. ". . . still breathing."

Without the glow of the dead wishes, Van couldn't quite follow her lips. Still, the relief on her face was clear.

She knelt beside the man in the white suit for a moment longer, murmuring something that Van couldn't catch. Then, slowly, she got to her feet.

"Until . . . and Gerda . . . call for help," she said, taking a step away. But there, she stopped, her head bowed, a frown tugging the features of her face.

"What is it?" Van asked. "You're not going to stay with him now, are you?"

"No," said Pebble quickly. "It's not that." She glanced around the room once more, the light from the windows catching her features. Van watched her face in the moonlight. "I just . . ." She turned to Van. "That giant Eater . . ."

Van nodded. "It must have been the one from the well. I saw it too."

"Did you feel it?" Pebble asked. "When it ate the wishes?"

Van nodded again. "It could have done anything. It could have destroyed this whole house. And us. But it didn't."

Pebble hesitated. She pulled her baggy coat tight around herself. "Maybe you're right," Van thought he heard her say. "About the Eaters. Maybe . . ."

They both kept still for a moment. A breeze swept in through the hole above, fluttering the ends of Van's hair.

Pebble glanced up at the night sky. "We should go."

They hurried down through the dark, quiet house.

Van waited in the foyer as Pebble unlocked the basement door and shouted instructions down to Hans and Gerda. Together, they stepped out the front door—straight into a line of waiting spikes.

Van and Pebble sprang backward, gasping. The row of Collectors, who had just been about to storm the house, sprang backward too.

"Pebble!" voices shouted. ". . . here! . . . all right!"

Van scanned the crowd. He spotted Nail, with Raduslav and Violetta, and Razor, and Eyelet, and Jack and many more. They were battered and tired, their nets ripped and their boots caked with mud. Several wore deep, bloody scratches. Two had arms wrapped in makeshift slings. But they were all alive.

"Pebble." Nail stepped to the front of the crowd. His voice was more ragged than Van had ever heard it. *"Thank goodness!"* He threw open his arms.

For the second time that night, Van watched Pebble disappear into a happy crowd. He caught bits of explanations and questions and apologies, and saw Pebble point up toward the ruined tower, telling the end of the story. Then she aimed her pointing hand at Van. Her face cracked into a smile.

Van felt himself being wrapped in someone's arms and pulled into the crowd. Hands patted his back and tousled his hair. Jack grinned down at him. Pebble squeezed his arm.

A warm, heavy palm landed on his shoulder.

"Van Markson," said Razor, bending close. "I believe I found something of yours."

He opened his other big, bloodstained hand to reveal a small blue hearing aid.

Van picked up the hearing aid. It looked undamaged. When he slid it into place, he found that—incredibly—it still worked. He looked up at Razor. "In that whole huge clearing, with everything that was going on, you saw this?"

Razor shrugged one big shoulder. "I'm good at spotting things others don't see." He smiled at Van, his scar curving, his black eyes bright. "I think that makes two of us."

Abruptly, Razor's face hardened. His eyes went sharp. He straightened to his full height, grabbing the hooks strapped to his back.

"*Eater,*" he growled.

The crowd of Collectors whirled into formation, readying weapons, grasping nets. They stared at the edge of the woods.

A large, misty shape drifted onto the edge of the lawn. Its eyes were wide. Its fuzzy ears twitched anxiously. Cradled in its arms was a silvery squirrel.

"It's Lemmy!" screamed Van. "Don't hurt it!"

He flung himself through the crowd. Halfway between the Wish Eater and the Collectors, he spun around, his arms spread, staring into the mass of sharpened metal.

The Collectors, ragged with injuries, waited. Their eyes narrowed. Their hands tightened around iron spikes.

"This is Lemmy," shouted Van, as steadily as he could. "It saved our lives tonight, mine and Pebble's and—"

"Of course it did," said Jack's sharp voice. "If you wished it."

"Not because we wished it," Van argued. "Because it *wanted to*. It has feelings of its own. It should get to make choices of its own. Wish Eaters aren't all bad. They're—they're just like *us*. They can do awful things, and they can do *good* things."

None of the Collectors moved.

None except for Pebble.

"It's true!" she shouted, charging out of the crowd and running to Van's side. "Lemmy saved us. Twice. And it saved Barnavelt too. None of us would be here right now without it!"

"That's right!" squeaked a small voice. Barnavelt craned over Lemmy's misty arm, calling down to the Collectors. "None of us would be here! And look—we're all here! Me, and Pebble, and Van, and me, and Lemmy, and me. Hey, Pebble! We're all here!"

Pebble held up her hands. Barnavelt leaped into them.

"I flew!" the squirrel told her. "I was flying, Pebble! Did you see me?"

"Pebble . . . ," said Nail warningly. "You know very well how dangerous Eaters can be."

"*Anyone* can be dangerous," argued Pebble. "Eaters have hurt us. And we've hurt them."

Lemmy drifted close, pressing up against Van's back. Van could feel the Eater's misty body quivering. He reached up to touch its side.

"You can't keep on doing this," said Van. "Hurting and scaring the Eaters and locking them all up forever, just because you're *afraid*." A few of the Collectors stiffened at this. Van pushed on, even though his voice shook. "It isn't right."

Pebble pressed her shoulder against his.

"It *isn't* right," she agreed. "It has to change, or—or I can't come back with you."

There was a stir in the crowd. Van turned to stare at her.

Pebble went on, her voice firm. "I wouldn't stay with Uncle Ivor, and I won't stay with you either. You're not just trying to keep everyone safe. You're trying to control things. If you do that to Lemmy . . . then I can't be a Collector anymore."

Nail stared at them for a moment. Then, slowly, he turned his eyes to Razor. The Collectors lowered their weapons.

"Very well," Nail announced. "We will discuss this further. Perhaps," he added dryly, "after we see how much damage Falborg's Eaters have done to the Collection in our absence."

"Okay." Pebble nodded sharply. "We'll discuss it."

"And Lemmy goes free," said Van. "Right? For good?"

Nail's mouth made a hard line, but his gaze was steady. "For good," he answered at last. "You have our word."

Van wrapped his arms around Lemmy. Misty softness brushed his skin. The Wish Eater gazed down at Van, a tiny smile seeming to uncurl on its face.

Beyond Lemmy's foggy body, Van could see the stars fading from the sky, the deep blue of night rinsing to the pale hue of dawn.

"I should get back to the Fox Den," he told Pebble. "My mother will worry."

Pebble nodded. Before Van could react, she threw her arms around him, squeezing him tight. Barnavelt's whiskers brushed his ear.

"Bye, Van Gogh," the squirrel whispered.

"Will I see you again?" Van asked as Pebble released him.

Pebble took a step back, pulling her bulky coat close. "We'll see," she said. "Keep your eyes open." She nodded to the Wish Eater behind him. "Goodbye, Lemmy."

Before Van could ask any more questions, his feet left the ground. From the Eater's arms, he watched Pebble and the rest of the Collectors dwindling away below him, the Falborg mansion shrinking until it was swallowed by trees. And then there was nothing beneath the soles of his shoes but the softly stirring forest.

Lemmy landed in the shadows behind the Fox Den's outdoor stage. Van slid out of the Eater's arms, filled with the same disappointed heaviness he always felt when a flight was over. The first time Lemmy had carried him, soaring over the rooftops of the city to leave him at the Greys' house, Van had thought that their goodbyes might have been for good. But now, with Nail's promise that Lemmy would remain free, Van hoped this wasn't a goodbye at all.

"Thank you, Lemmy," he said instead. "Thank you."

The Eater gave him one last tiny smile. It turned and floated into the trees, its cloudy body setting their leaves swaying gently. In a blink, it was gone from sight.

But just because he couldn't see it didn't mean it wasn't there.

Van took a deep, long breath. With Lemmy—and Mr. Falborg's released Eaters, and the ancient thing from the bottom of the well—all waiting somewhere in it, the world seemed scattered with more magic than ever. Like a big shady park where a thousand lost treasures might hide.

"Giovanni!" His mother's voice rang through the dimness.

Van whirled around.

His mother stood on a rise near the festival stage, craning in his direction. On the dark grass behind her were two other figures, both of them sitting up. Moving. Alive.

Van raced across the grass. He hurled himself into his mother's arms, the emerald-green dress and the smell of lilies enveloping him.

"Giovanni, what are you doing out here?" she asked, releasing him. "You should have been in bed *hours* ago!"

"I just—" Van improvised. "I noticed all the lights out here, so I came out to see what was going on."

His mother nodded, looking slightly dazed. "Yes, we've had several little emergencies. The reception tent caught fire. There was some sort of altercation in the driveway. Peter was injured by a falling light. It's all been a bit . . . chaotic."

Van looked down at the grass beside them. Mr. Grey sat with his arm around Peter's shoulders, looking rumpled and grass stained. Peter leaned against his father. A small bandage covered the side of his head.

"Are you okay?" Van asked, crouching beside him.

"I'm *fine*," said Peter. His voice was irritated, but Van could see the pleased smile at the corners of his mouth. "My dad's just making a fuss."

". . . not sure . . . *fine*," said Mr. Grey, with an anxious look at Peter's head. "I'd like to get . . . directly to the doctor . . . soon . . . the city."

"Dad. Seriously." Peter sighed as his father rose and pulled him to his feet. "It barely even hurts."

Van tapped Peter's arm. "I'm glad you're okay," he said.

Peter met Van's eyes. As his father guided him away, he turned back to flash Van the devil's horns, along with another small smile.

"What a strange night," sighed Van's mother, watching them go.

"Yeah," agreed Van.

"I was certain that this place would be safer than the city." She shook her head at the wreckage of the Fox Den grounds. "Perhaps our curse has followed us."

"Maybe," said Van. "Or maybe it's not really a curse at all." He slipped his hand into his mother's. "Maybe . . . maybe it means that bad things happen, but we're always okay in the end."

His mother gazed down at him for a moment. "Yes," she said, more softly than usual. "We have everything we need." She gave Van's hand a squeeze. "Now, both of us ought to get straight to bed. *Andiamo.*"

They set off down the path, Van's mother walking without a trace of her limp, and Van glancing up at the sky where, one by one, the last stars were winking out.

23
Wish You Were Here

Winter was sneaking up on the city.

The trees still shook clusters of gold and brown leaves, and a few hardy flowers still tumbled from window boxes, but the air had an icy edge to it. There were fewer lost sunglasses and more rumpled tissues in the litter that gathered along the street.

Late one autumn evening, Van Markson and his mother strolled along a quiet sidewalk. They had just come from having dinner at the Greys', where Van's mother and Mr. Grey and a few opera friends had lingered around the table while Van and Peter had fired lasers at alien ships upstairs. Now they were on their way home.

They had been back in the city for two days. The season at the Fox Den was over, and Van's mother had a recording contract and several holiday concerts to give. Returning to the city—to the same apartment that had been theirs before—felt strange to Van, who had never come back to the same place twice. It felt like trying to slip into your favorite sweater from three years ago, finding that you've grown too big to fit inside it anymore.

Van wasn't sure where he would fit now.

The Collectors had to know he was back. They knew every corner of the city, every birthdate, every address. But he'd seen no sign of them so far—not even a suspicious raven on his windowsill. Maybe they didn't need him anymore.

And no matter how hard he looked, he hadn't caught a glimpse of Lemmy either. But he wasn't going to stop watching.

"Giovanni, " said his mother, touching his arm as they passed a corner grocery. Van looked up. "I need to stop for milk and coffee. Our kitchen is still half bare."

"Can I stay out here?" asked Van.

"All right," said his mother. "But stay right in front of the shop, and don't move. I'll be just a moment."

She swept through the door.

Van stood alone on the quiet sidewalk. The air

smelled like leaves and smoke. Between the tall brick buildings around him, the sky was a deep navy blue. He gazed up, searching for falling stars and flickering wishes, the magic that might be hidden anywhere . . . but this time, even though he waited and waited, there were no lights, and no falling stars. A flash of silvery gray swept past the corner of his eye. Van spun toward it, scanning the rooftops where it had appeared. Whatever it was had vanished. *Maybe it was only a wisp of steam,* he told himself, his heart sinking back down in his chest. *Maybe it wasn't a Wish Eater at all.*

Maybe his time as part of that magical, hidden world was over.

He turned his eyes to the sidewalk. Cigarette butts. A flattened straw. And peering out from behind a row of trash cans, a pair of glimmering eyes.

"Hey," whispered a voice.

Van froze.

"It's not easy to get you alone," the voice went on. "I've been chasing you back and forth through this city like a fool for the past two days."

A cat slipped out from between the trash cans.

A long-haired gray cat with a disdainful look on its face.

"Renata?" Van whispered.

"I told you," the cat snapped, "call me *Chuck*." Mr. Falborg's former pet padded closer, her plumy tail swishing behind her. "Renata is just the name Mr. Fancy-pants had engraved on my jeweled collar. A collar I refused to wear, by the way."

"Are you . . . are you living with Mr. Falborg again?" Van asked anxiously. "Is he in the city right now? Did *he* tell you to follow me?"

"You think I'd obey him if he did?" the cat snorted. "I'm not a bloodhound." She gave her whiskers a lazy stroke. "Of course not. Besides, Falborg's city house is for sale. He won't be coming back here anytime soon."

"Oh." Van exhaled deeply. "Then . . . why are you following me?"

"Well, I wasn't *just* following you," said the cat. "This neighborhood is one of my regular haunts. The stray cat act pays well, if you know how to work it." She gave her whiskers a last pat. "As long as I was heading this way already, I agreed to do a favor for an old friend."

The cat turned and pawed a square of paper out from behind the trash cans.

It was a postcard.

On its front was a sketch of a small, dingy, gray office

wedged between two other buildings. It was the kind of place that certainly didn't belong on a postcard. It was the kind of place that most people wouldn't give a second glance. It was the kind of place that only someone like Van would notice.

"You mean, Pebble—" The joy swelling in Van's chest almost cut off his breath. "She sent this to me? The Collectors haven't forgotten about me?"

The cat looked at Van with canny eyes. "How do you think you ended up back in this city, kid? A coincidence?" She tilted her head. "I've got to run. The Meyers had fish tonight, and they'll be looking for someone small and pretty to feed the scraps to."

With a swish of her plumy gray tail, Chuck vanished into the shadows.

Van picked up the postcard with shaking fingers. The light of a nearby streetlamp fell around him, its beam dotted by a falling whirl of leaves. He turned the postcard over. He read the words printed there, and then he read them again and again, smiling wider every time.

WISH YOU WERE HERE.

Acknowledgments

I owe a world of thanks to all the hard of hearing and deaf students who spent time with me as I started work on these books: Austyn, Noah, Brian, Kennedy, Dalina, Gifty, Dexter, Amber V., Amber H., Ella, Cara, Nikki, and Maddie. Giant thanks also to expert readers Angela Dahlen and Linda Lytle for their time and their invaluable feedback, and to teachers Shanna Swenson, Angela Dahlen, and Amanda Kline. These stories wouldn't exist without all of you. Thank you for letting me try to bottle a little bit of your light.

A thousand thanks to my amazing editor, Martha Mihalick, for the time, the support, the vision, and the pushing when I've needed it. To Lois Adams, Laaren Brown, Virginia Duncan, Paul Zakris, Ann Dye,

Acknowledgments

Robby Imfeld, Kris Kam, Haley George, Katie Heit, and everyone else at Greenwillow: thank you for shaping these books into what they've become.

Danielle Chiotti, Michael Stearns, and everyone at Upstart Crow Literary: I can't tell you just how grateful I am, but I'll keep trying with every new book.

My critique group—Anne Greenwood Brown, Connie Kingrey Anderson, Lauren Peck, and Jennifer Kaul—gets me out of my house and out of my head. Writing can be lonely work, but it's a lot less lonely with all of you. Thank you, thank you, thank you.

Anne Ursu, Adam Gidwitz, Will Alexander, and Jonathan Auxier: your support means more than I can say. (And speaking of support, any writer who isn't part of the Minnesota kid lit community is missing out. Just saying.)

I'll never stop feeling out-of-this-world lucky to see my books in readers' hands. In my head, I'm thanking every single bookshop and bookseller who helps make this happen, but on paper, I'll have to single out just a few local wonder-workers: Red Balloon in St. Paul: Valley Bookseller in Stillwater, Minnesota: Fox Den Books in River Falls, Wisconsin; and Fair Trade Books in Red Wing, Minnesota. Thanks also to all the book bloggers, bookstagrammers, librarians, book club facilitators, and teachers who connect stories with readers. You make the world magical.

Thanks to all the music teachers, singers, coaches, and professors I've been lucky enough to learn from, and thanks to my favorite opera singer, Jack Swanson. (You know I steal little bits of your life for these stories, right?)

Mom and Dad, Dan, Katy, Alex, and all the grandparents and aunts and uncles and cousins and in-laws who have supported me, helped me, and loved me: thank you forever.

And most of all, thanks to Ryan and Beren. Life with you two is more wonderful than anything I could make up.